Love Don't Make Cents

V. MARIE

A little inspiration...

The 50th Law
=
Fear Nothing

A single principle coined by
Curtis "50 Cent" Jackson.

DEDICATION

To dreams.
To dream is to live.
To live is to live.
Live your dreams.

CHAPTER ONE

"So, tell us a little bit about yourself."

It was the opening line for the interview of a lifetime and Heather drew a blank. Hip Hop journalist and writing extraordinaire, Heather Grand sat on the opposite side of the interview for a new job that she had been dying for. This was the moment she had been waiting for and all she could think about was absolutely nothing. She stared off into space for what seemed like an entire time zone before she came to.

"Ms. Grand?" Mr. Fleuron spoke breaking

Heather's daze.

"Yes, I'm sorry Mr. Fleuron. I am just a little nervous."

"It's fine," chimed in a woman who wasn't quite a woman, "take your time." She waved her hand at the air.

After a few moments, Heather received a second wind and ran off her resume with overly impressive responses to the two interviewers.

Mr. Daniel Fleuron, the CEO of Musiq Magazine, owned the hottest hip hop print magazine on the shelves. His sidekick, Mandy Innis, who was born as Randy, was the one running the show. Heather had tried to get this interview for the past year and when it finally arrived and she nearly bombed it.

"Well, Ms. Grand, we will call you."

The famous line had met the airwaves. She didn't get the job.

"Thank you for the opportunity." Heather

replied as she shook both of their hands before leaving the interview.

"How did it go?" Justice asked.

"I think I blew it." Heather replied.

"Why?" Justice was surprised.

These two had been attached at the hip and best friends since they were in diapers, literally. Their mothers gave birth on the same day and met during recovery. Their moms became fast friends, so Heather and Justice were destined to be the same. They were like twins almost. When one was down, the other was down and when one was happy, the other was happy. Justice knew something went wrong when she didn't get a call after the interview.

"I froze."

"What do you mean, you froze?"

"I mean what I said. They asked me to tell them

about myself and I froze."

"But that is the easiest question in the interview."

"I know and that is what made it so bad."

"What did they say at the end?"

"That they'd call me."

"Oh, no."

"Exactly."

Heather quickly changed the subject because she did not want to talk about the interview any longer.

"Are you coming home tonight?"

"No, I am going to stay over my baby's house tonight." Justice answered.

Justice's attempt to cheer up Heather didn't work, so the two said their goodbyes for the night.

The following week, Heather went back to her boring column job at Hip Hop Vibe. It was an exciting job at first. She wrote about hip hop and R&B artists' careers. Now that shc had practically written all she could about some of the hottest artists, she was ready to move on to something new. She wanted something different. Heather was ready for some excitement in her career.

ONE MONTH LATER

Just when Heather had stopped interviewing for other jobs, she finally got a hit on the one she wanted.

"Heather Grand." Heather answered her phone.

"Ms. Grand, this is Ms. Innis from Musiq. How are you?"

Heather's heart nearly hopped out of her chest, but she quickly gathered her composure. "I'm fine."

"I was calling to see if you are still interested in a position."

"Of course, I am."

"Well, come by on Monday and we'll talk about an offer and some other details."

"Absolutely."

"See you at 8 am sharp."

Monday could not arrive fast enough. The entire weekend seemed to drag on, especially since Justice was starting to spend more time at her boyfriend's place, leaving Heather to entertain herself.

When she arrived at Musiq, Heather contemplated whether she had made the best decision on what to wear. She definitely did not want to dress like she was in the field, but she didn't want to over do it either. If she stayed in the middle, she could get away with a pencil skirt and a tapered blouse that accentuated her waistline. She ran her hands down her skirt as she stood at the elevator.

"Good morning, Ms. Grand." Mr. Fleuron greeted her as he approached the elevator.

"Good morning, sir."

"Oh, don't start with that sir, shit. Just call me Dan."

"Okay…Dan."

The elevator opened and Dan allowed Heather to step in first. No one else came in with them. Heather immediately felt the awkward silence between them.

"This job you're taking on will have you traveling 100%. I hope that doesn't scare you. If so, you can decide to go back home right now."

"Well, uh no. I haven't heard about the position at all, but traveling will not be a problem.

"Good. I need someone who looks like you and has your talent in the field capturing moments and stories, almost like paparazzi."

"Paparazzi?" Heather giggles.

"Something funny?" Dan didn't crack a smile.

"No." Heather got straight faced and looked forward.

The elevator dinged and the doors slowly opened and Heather exhaled as she stepped directly into the Musiq office.

The Musiq corporate office was located on the fiftieth floor of a Manhattan building. Heather had only been beyond the conference room once for an industry meeting some years ago. She could not believe her chance had finally arrived for her to start writing for her idol publication.

"Wait here. I'll get Ms. Innis." Dan walked behind a secure door. Moments later, Ms. Innis came through the door as bubbly as ever.

"Good morning, Ms. Grand. Right this way."

Heather followed Ms. Innis through the door to a much quieter than expected office. Heather looked around at all of the empty cubicles and offices. Ms. Innis turned several corners and walked into a glass enclosed office with a view of Manhattan's upper east side.

"Have a seat. I'll be right back. Can I get you

some coffee or anything?"

"No. I'm fine, thank you."

Ms. Innis returned moments later with a file in her hand.

"Thank you for coming to this meeting. We did like you during the interview; however, we went through a little re-organization over the past month with staff and positions so it took us some time to get back with you."

"I see." Heather was ready to take notes, but wrote nothing yet.

Ms. Innis babbled on about the re-organization and all of the unproductive writers they had to lay off and the new positions they had to create to ignite the magazine for a new age fan base. She said that social media had created a culture of people who expected to be in the know of everything the celebrities were doing. Musiq had been the pioneer in a lot of areas, yet were falling behind with the social media aspect.

"This is where you come in, young lady."

"Okay." Heather leaned in.

"We're offering you a Tour Journalist position. You will be traveling on tour with specific artists that we have relationships with. You're going to become their personal paparazzi. You are not a gossiper nor is your job to get any compromising stories from the artist. You are expected to help write the stories that help sell the music without all the drama. Based on our research, our target audience actually reads our magazine."

"Sounds kinda boring, though."

Ms. Innis raised her eyebrow in surprise, "How so?"

"It sounds like I'll be tagging along, but I am only writing about twenty percent of what really goes on. I wouldn't want to read about that and I surely couldn't write it. Look, I am a hip hop journalist. I write what is hot and what's not. I can't just right about the "what's not" stuff."

"I appreciate your outspokenness, but this is the scope."

"I'm sorry, but I would like to modify it a bit."

Ms. Innis looked appalled at the suggestion. "Look Ms. Grand, I know your work is impeccable. I think that you can do this as is. Mr. Fleuron is not going to have you come in here and change everything around."

"You're right, Ms. Innis, my work does speak for itself, but that is because my editors have given me creative license to work my magic. I cannot accept this position without some flexibility."

"One moment." Ms. Innis stood up and left the office.

Heather could hear chatter back and forth between Dan and Ms. Innis, and since it was as quiet as a church in the office, it didn't sound like Ms. Innis was winning the debate. Moments passed, then Dan and Ms. Innis entered the office.

"So I hear there is some concern about the

scope." Dan said.

"Just a little." Heather confirmed.

"Well I will tell you straight. This is a new position. We're trying something new and we want it to be successful. If you think we can stand to tweak it, then let's give it a try."

Heather beamed with excitement.

"But, if you fail, then you're fired. Are we clear?" Dan said firmly.

"Yes, sir…I mean, Dan."

"Mandy, tighten this up and get her booked for the Mark B. tour. It starts Sunday in Las Vegas and we have loads of paperwork to do."

Heather's heart nearly stopped. Her first gig was with the one and only Mark B. James. He has been her number one artist since her senior year of college.

"Will do." Mandy nodded to Dan.

Dan left and the door remained open.

"Where is everyone?" Heather motioned to the

empty office.

"It's a company holiday."

"Company holiday?"

"Yea, after we cover a major industry event for two weeks straight and overwork the staff, we give them a day off. It's a paid day of recovery. It will be bananas in here tomorrow, preparing for the ETA. You know, the Entertainment Television Awards is in a few months."

"Yea. I know."

"Don't worry, you'll be covering the event."

"Wait, I thought I would be on the road, 100%."

"You will be. The event is in Atlanta this year and from what the circuit is saying, Mark B. James is up for a few awards and his tour runs right into the schedule. He'll be there and so will you."

"Wait, so why isn't someone from his label actually doing this job?"

"They tried that and think we'll do a better job. Besides, Mr. Fleuron and the CEO over at

Retrospect Records are working on this collaboratively. You will have full cooperation from Mark B. while he's on this world tour."

"Well, I have a lot of work to do. Will I have an office onsite?"

"An office? Honey, child, no. You'll be in a cubicle."

"Uh, I need an office. That's my only other request."

"This position is a level M, so I guess we can pull that off."

"Speaking of salary. The original position was posted at 75K. Is that still the offer?" Heather had her pen and paper ready.

"Yes, that is still the rate. There is a sign on bonus and stipend included since you'll practically be living out of a suitcase for a while. You'll need to prepare to be away from home except or unless the tour has a break in schedule. So get new luggage and travel size everything." Ms. Innis smiled while signing some documents.

"Okay. This will be interesting." Heather said.

"You don't say. Mark B. and his PA can be a handful." Ms. Innis pushed a contract across the desk for Heather to sign.

As she signed the contract, "Funny, I didn't get that vibe from him when we met at ETA a couple years ago."

"Times have changed." Ms. Innis said.

"So, what do I do when I am not touring?" Heather wanted to change the subject.

"You'll always be touring, but if there is a break in the tour unexpected, then we'll put you on a tour already in progress."

"Oh."

Heather asked no more questions. She had a lot of prep work to do before her trip. This was it. Her big shot.

"Alright, tomorrow when you come in, I'll send you over to human resources for all of the other necessary paperwork and introduce you to your administrative support."

"Thank you, Ms. Innis."

"Well, now that you are part of the team, you can call me Mandy."

"Thanks, Mandy."

"This is a huge leap. Don't blow it." Mandy said.

"I won't."

"Jus!"

Justice came running out of the bathroom with her bath towel covering her body.

"What?!"

"I got the job."

"What job?"

"Musiq!"

"What!" Justice screamed, jumped up and down nearly dropped her towel.

"They called me back."

"When?! Why didn't you tell me?"

"You were over Darrin's this weekend and I didn't want to bother you."

"Oh my goodness. So what is the job?"

"It's a tour journalist."

"A what?"

"I'm going to be a personal journalist to an artist while they are on tour."

"How did you manage to get that type of gig?"

"They had a journalist position posted but they didn't throw in all that extra until they called me back. Apparently, they did a re-org and they needed to change up some of their content."

"That's awesome, Heather. When do you start?"

"Tomorrow, but I go on tour next week."

"With who?"

"Mark B."

"Oh my! Mark B. Your Mark B?"

"Yes, I know. I don't know how I am going to

maintain myself. I was nervous when she told me."

"This is huge!"

"Tell me about it."

"I can't wait to brag about your column."

"Well, let me get started first."

"So wait…you'll be traveling?"

"Yes. I'll be gone for a while. Do you think you can hold down the place while I'm gone?"

"Oh, sure. You know where I'll be."

"I only have a few days to prepare for the trip so I'll be locked up in my room kinda thinking about how I'm going to pull this off."

"What do you mean? What do you have to write about?"

"That's just it. They wanted me to only write about the good stuff, sorta blah blah blah stuff, but I told them, hip hop artists are more dramatic and I need freedom to be creative."

"And…what did they say?"

"They are giving me one shot."

"I am sure you'll nail it. You always do."

"Thanks, sis."

"I am going to leave you to it. I have an industry dinner party to go to tonight."

"You have fun."

Justice walked with a purpose back to the bathroom and Heather headed to her room happy that she wasn't going to that industry party tonight. Heather was not a huge fan of industry parties, but she had to go to them when invited. Justice's boyfriend was an entertainment attorney, so he went to the events to support clients and to scout new ones. Justice was a New York City news anchor who frequented a lot of industry events just because. Ever since Justice started dating Darrin, whom she met at one of those parties, Heather was relieved of going to parties just to accompany her best friend.

In her loft master bedroom, Heather found a comfortable spot near the window to start her journal for this job. In other jobs, she spent most of her time surfing the net and being around town at different events to cover a story. This is her first real column where everything in it will be hers. It had to be right.

By that Friday, Heather had all of her ducks in a row. A meeting with Mark B. and his PA was scheduled at the Musiq office in preparation for the tour. Heather was about to meet her favorite hip hop artist and spend the next six months writing about his life.

CHAPTER TWO

Heather sat at the conference table with her new bosses and administrative staff. They awaited the arrival of Mark B. They were more than fashionably late, as usual. Heather was prepared to take on this project like a new born baby. Nothing would get in the way of her making this the best hip hop column in the industry, including Mark B. James.

When the receptionist escorted Mark B. and his personal assistant into the room, Heather was ready for "game on". Mark B. took a seat at the head of the table and his assistant sat across from Heather. Everyone said their quick greetings. The newbie in the room, Heather, took the opportunity to set the tone, when the introduction came around to her.

"Good afternoon, Mr. James and Ms. Oni, I am Heather Grand, your tour journalist." The entire room turned to look at Heather. She stood and walked over to Mark B. and Ms. Oni and properly shook their hands.

She continued, "I am new to the team, but I am not new to the game. If we have a meeting scheduled for 1 o'clock, please be on time or expect it to be canceled. The success of this column is all of our responsibility; but primarily yours and mine," she looked directly at Mark B. "We will be attached at the hip for some time; so, the next time you will be late, for another meeting, please call me." Heather slid her card on the table for them both, and she took her seat and said, "Now, let's get started."

Dan raised an eyebrow at Ms. Innis in complete surprise at Heather's introduction. He was caught off guard by it all and had to clear his throat to break the ice.

"Thank you, Ms. Grand for your introduction. Let's get this show on the road." He chuckled at his pun.

For the next couple of hours, they mapped out the schedule for interviewing during the tour. Heather had already planned what she wanted to do for the column, but she had to let the bosses do their thing. When they got on the road it was going to be up to her and Mark B. to make this column come alive.

"Mr. James, I understand that you have a personal life and I will hope to have one from time to time on this tour. If ever you need us to take a break or there are times where you will not want coverage, please let me know in advance so that I may plan accordingly. After today, I'll become your living shadow and will do my best to remain in the shadows. We can collaborate on the pieces; but please understand that this is to drive sales and create new fans."

"Ms. Grand, I appreciate your structure and I will be all yours." Mark B. said in a carefree tone.

"Great." Heather said as she started to gather her things.

"I think we're ready to wrap up. Any other questions before we let the train leave the station?" Dan asked.

"I think we're good here." Answered Ms. Oni.

Mark B. and the others shook their heads in agreement.

"Then we're adjourned." Dan said.

"Actually, can I have a moment with you, alone?" Mark B. said to Heather as everyone else was preparing to leave.

Heather sat back down and opened her notebook. "Sure."

The rest of the room cleared and it was just the two of them.

"What can I do for you, Mr. James?" Heather was confident on the outside, and jiggling with nervousness on the inside.

"First, please stop calling me that. You can call me Mark or B, but no more Mr. James. I am not your boss nor will I try to be."

"Okay. Anything else?"

"Will you always be this uptight?"

"Uptight?"

"Yes, I like to have fun. I like to party and I hope that I don't have to start being someone else for you to make this a good column."

"Don't worry about how I do my job. If you do yours, then that will make my life much easier."

"So, I guess that was a 'yes', then."

"If you want to know if I am a fan or if I am going to let my hair down on the job, then the answer is, no. I love hip hop and I love your music;

however, this is my job and I take it very seriously. Don't worry about me. Most of the time you won't even know I'm there."

"If you say so." Mark let out a sigh.

"Is that it?" Heather asked.

"I think so. I'll see you on the hanger."

"Hanger?"

"Yes, you'll be flying out on my jet."

"No tour bus?" Heather said sarcastically.

"Yea, right. Those days are over, Ms. Grand."

"Of course they are. What was I thinking? And please call me, Heather."

"Now…we're getting somewhere." Mark smiled.

Heather returned the gesture and gathered her things and confirmed, "The hanger it is."

Heather and Mark walked out of the meeting together. Heather went to her office to organize some files before leaving. Ms. Innis was right on her heels. She knocked on Heather's door.

"What was that about?"

"What?" Heather pretended not to know.

"That little private meeting with Mark. Is everything okay?"

"Yes. Everything is fine. He just wanted me to lose the bad girl attitude."

"I agree." Ms. Innis said in a serious tone.

"As I told Mr. James, I do my job my way. I do not need him nor you telling me how professional I should be."

Ms. Innis looked indignant at Heather's response as she turned and walked away. Heather knew that she had just picked a fight with the wrong person, but she was not going to keep being told how to do her job. She was ready for this and it was show time.

The morning of the trip, Ms. Oni contacted Heather and told her to be ready for the driver by 8 am. That was news to Heather because she was supposed to get her own transportation to the airport. When the car arrived, she walked down to the curb with her luggage and looked back at her brownstone apartment like it was the last time she would see it.

When the driver stepped out to open her door, Heather was already opening it. She was not used to this type of treatment and she was going to tell Mark that. She did not want to start being treated like a celebrity. That wasn't her style. She was used to doing things that normal people did. To her surprise, Mark was in the car. It looked like she would get her chance right away to set him straight.

"Hello, Heather." Mark greeted.

"Hi, Mark." Heather said.

"I hope the transportation change was not a problem." Mark smiled.

"It's not a problem, but I don't want it to be a habit."

"A habit? What do you mean?"

"I am not a celebrity and I don't want to get all of this special treatment."

"Special treatment?"

"You know, cars, chauffeurs, private jets…it's just not my thing."

"Well, I'm sorry Heather but this is the job. If you are going to be my shadow, then you'll have to be treated the way I am treated. You'll have to adjust. Like it or not."

Heather didn't reply. It was useless. She already knew how celebrities lived. She knew how much money they spent on frivolous things and she didn't like it. She grew up in a big house, fancy cars, and five star restaurants, but when she moved out and started living on her own, those things were not important.

"Are we cool?" Mark said as the driver merged

into traffic headed to La Guardia.

"We're cool."

"Good." Mark put on his earbuds and laid his head back on the headrest.

Heather sat watching the traffic and wondered how much longer she could keep her composure. Her idol and fantasy love of all times was sitting inches away from her and she could not let him know how she felt. The career opportunity of a lifetime was in her hand and all she had to do was keep her head in the game and not allow any distractions get in the way of her job.

On the jet, Heather made herself comfortable in the rear with her laptop. She was already building her story for the launch article. All she had to do was start writing. The beginning of her new journey was taking off, literally…ready or not.

"Are you okay?"

Heather was startled by Mark's voice. She was deep in thought as she worked on her introduction for the first article.

"Yes."

"I hope I didn't scare you."

"Not at all. I was actually starting the introduction for the first story."

"Really? How are you doing that and you have only said about two words to me since we've met."

"Mark, I know more about you than you think."

Mark raised in eyebrow.

"Is that so?"

"I did not become the best hip hop journalist by not knowing about all of you."

"Okay, Ms. Hip Hop. Who is your favorite artist?"

"Oh, I don't like to talk about favorites to other artists. No offense. I have my favorites for the business, but then I have personal favorites and both times I have let the cat out of the bag, it turned into a debate."

"I can see how that could turn out badly for you.

I love music and I have my favorites, but like you, I don't talk about them like that."

"So, I'm off the hook?" Heather teased.

"You got me."

"Good, because I'd hate to hurt your feelings by not choosing you as my favorite."

"Ha!"

"You thought I would pick you, didn't you?"

"No, I was just wondering why you'd take on this type of job unless you really like hip hop or me – that much."

"I really like hip hop." Heather teased.

"Got me, again."

"I am as quick on my feet as you are."

"That is good to know. All jokes aside, these tours can be pretty brutal. Fans are going to be jealous of you, my staff will be pushy and the hours will be torture."

Heather took in all of the fair warnings and knew that he was right. Fans will think that they are dating, the staff will think she is someone they can order around, and the hustle and bustle of the tour schedule would be crazy. 10-4. Tell her something she didn't know.

"Where is Ms. Oni?" Heather asked.

"She is not going to be in Vegas with us. She will be joining us in LA. It will be you and I mostly. Will that be a problem?"

"No. As long as you don't think I am your PA, we're cool."

"I'd never do that. I have a PA coming in to assist both of us."

"Us?"

"I told you. You're my shadow. If you need something, then I got you."

"Mark, you really don't have to do that. I am getting paid for this job so I don't want you to spend any extra on me."

"I thought we had this talk already."

"I know, but…"

"But, nothing."

"How long before we get there?" Heather decided to change the subject.

"A couple of hours, why?"

"I want to take a nap. I didn't sleep too well last night."

"Okay, well you can go through that door and take a nap."

Mark pointed at the door beyond the last seat. Heather was surely going to take him up on the offer as she gathered her things and went through the door. On the other side of the cabin was a mini suite. Heather took off her shoes and laid across the bed and dozed off.

When she started to wake up she turned over and found that Mark had made himself comfortable on the opposite side. He was sleeping soundly next to her. Heather watched him sleep so peacefully. She thought he never slept as much as he seemed to be on the go. A smile cracked through her lips as she admired the view laying next her. An announcement from the pilot startled and woke him up.

"Oh, shit." Mark said as he sat up quickly.

"What's wrong?"

"I was supposed to wake up before you."

Heather still laid in the same position that was facing him.

"And why is that?"

"I'm not supposed to sleep with my journalist."

"Ha ha, very funny."

"Seriously. I don't want you to get the wrong idea."

"Mark, lay back down. It's no big deal."

He obliged the offer and laid back down. This time Heather sat up and started to put on her shoes.

"Where are you going?"

"We're landing soon. I need to freshen up."

"I hope you're not getting up because of me."

"Of course not. You stay there as long as you

need. I was awake already."

"Good." Mark said and closed his eyes.

Heather had to hurry and get away from Mark before he got her too excited. The scent of his cologne alone was enough to get her wet, so the fact that she was laying in the same bed with him was more than she could handle.

Another announcement from the cockpit made Heather hurry up in the bathroom. A little power lipstick and a splash of perfume was enough to get her through the day. On the way out of the bathroom, she ran into Mark as he passed by without a shirt on, "Excuse me." Heather said.

"No, excuse me. I have to remember I have a guest."

"It's fine. I'll just walk around without my top on and see how well you can handle that."

"What a sight to be seen."

"It was a joke."

"Not to me."

They both laughed off the innuendo and started toward their seats for landing. Heather looked out at the sun that had started to lean toward the tip of the mountains of Las Vegas. She began to think about what she was getting herself into. Men were not her strong suit and men she worked with had definitely been recipes for disasters. She had to keep her head in the game. When the flight landed, Mark looked over to her and said, "I hope you're ready for this. Let's do it."

CHAPTER THREE

"Are you ready Las Vegas?!" Mark yelled to the crowd of fans from the massive platform. A thunderous roar filled the arena of Mark B. James fans. Flashing lights and pyrotechnics exploded and the music blared from the surround sound speakers. Heather watched the show from backstage. Mark came to check on her between sets.

"You good?" He put his sweaty arm around her shoulder and watched one of the artists on his same label do a set.

"I am. Are you enjoying yourself?" Heather

asked moving his sweaty arm from around her shoulder.

"Oh, my bad!" he laughed. "So are you working now or was that a personal question?" Mark said sarcastically.

"I am always working."

"Well in that case, I am having a ball. Write that down!"

Heather raised a brow at the first part of his response and laughed at the latter.

"Look, I know you're going to write a lot of things that fans like to hear, but I have to tell you, there are times when I want to be normal, too."

"Normal?"

"Yea, like you. Look at you. You can stand here watch the show, leave here in peace and no one will bother you."

"But that is what being a celebrity is all about."

"I know that, trust me."

"Do you want to give it up?"

"No. Look at those fans. The smiles on their faces are priceless. How can I take that away from them?"

"Good answer." Heather said. "So, being a celebrity gives you that sense of obligation, now?"

"Something like that."

"That's noble."

"Ha! Noble. I just wanted to make music and money. This celebrity shit is just part of that package. It's the good with the not so bad." Mark concluded.

"Touché."

The concert was about to end and Mark went out for the final set. The entire crowd roared when he entered the stage. Even Heather put a smile on her face when the anticipated hits from his first album closed out the show.

Heather was exhausted on the first day. She took a lot of notes, but she was in no shape to write anything that night. The after party was at a Las

Vegas club on the strip. It was definitely not something she looked forward to attending, but she had to go.

The music was loud. The club was packed and the fans and guests were all over Mark B. trying to get a photo. He was very humble and tried to get pictures with everyone until his security had to move him to the VIP section. Heather followed closely behind the crew, but was being pushed and tugged on by the crowd. She was falling further behind until she felt someone securely grab her hand to pull her through the mangled crowd. It was Mark B. He turned and looked back to meet her eyes. He nodded that he had her. She was now safely encapsulated between Mark and the security team.

Upstairs in the VIP room, it was a nice open space with other celebrities. It was much quieter and the wait staff walked around with trays offering hor'devours. Heather saw an opportunity to sit back and relax.

"Sorry about that back there." Mark turned to Heather as she was already eyeing a spot to sit.

"About what?" Heather asked shyly.

"About that chaos. Are you okay?" Mark was apologetic.

"I am now."

"Yeah, I forgot to introduce you to the tour security detail. They know now that you are one of us."

"Yeah, thank you."

"I won't be here long. We'll be going back to the hotel in about an hour. We just need to take a few pictures."

"I am fine."

"Aight, go mingle. I'll find you when I am ready to go." Mark said.

Heather did just the opposite. She found a quiet corner and pulled out her notebook. She watched the crowd of A-list celebrities and made note of how Mark B. worked the crowd. There were a lot of supermodel type women in the party – they all knew Mark B. Heather was definitely the plain Jane in the room. She wore comfortable jeans, a t-shirt, and sneakers. Her shoulder length hair was pulled back in a ponytail and absolutely no make up.

By the time Mark B. was ready to go Heather was already on yawn number seven. She was exhausted, but she managed to hang in there for the night. This new schedule would take some getting used to, she thought.

On the way to the car, Heather asked, "Well, how do you think the night went?"

"I had a blast, didn't you?" Mark was still hyped.

"I was in work mode. I didn't really mingle."

"Why not? You have to loosen up."

"This takes some getting used to. You've been on the go since we landed. I don't see how you do it." Heather chuckled.

When they arrived at the hotel, the security went

inside to get their rooms. When the security team came to the limousine, Mark B. stepped out to speak to them. He tapped on the window to get Heather's attention. Heather rolled down the window.

"There's been a problem with the rooms."

"What kind of problem?" Heather rolled her eyes.

"Apparently they overbooked the hotel and your room was bumped since you didn't check in earlier."

"Bumped?" Heather was disappointed and the exhaustion she felt was about to put her over her patience limit.

"Don't worry. I have the residential suite and it's a two bedroom. You can just stay with me tonight, unless you want me to book you at another hotel."

"No. I'll stay. I can't wait any longer. I am really tired."

Mark smiled, pulled the door open, and reached in to take her hand. "Right this way."

The suite was on the fiftieth floor of the Slender Hotel. It was a cylinder shaped hotel and the suite was designed to have a view of the city from anywhere in the room. It had a rotating floor that was controlled by remote.

"I hope you're okay with this. If Oni was here, this would not have happened. I apologize."

"It's fine. I should have checked my own reservation. I just assumed it was booked with yours."

"It was booked by your office, but I think we'll book it from now on."

Still standing in the foyer, "Where is my room?" Heather looked around the plush room.

"You can sleep in that one," he pointed to the master bedroom on the left, "and I'll sleep in that one," as he pointed to the room on the right.

"See you in the morning." Heather said.

"I will be out here watching television for a while. I need to unwind."

"Where are the groupies that try to beat your door down?" Heather teased.

"I pay a lot of money to keep them out of my room. I don't need random chicks in and out of my room. Trust me, I've had my share of thirsty booty."

"Thirsty booty?" Heather laughed.

"Yea, thirsty. You know the types."

"Of course. I saw plenty tonight at that party."

"Exactly. I am good right here, with you."

Mark B. walked over to Heather and planted a soft kiss on her forehead. Heather did not move. She couldn't. The warmth from his body was invading her and she was waking up. Mark didn't move either. Heather felt like he wanted her to respond to the kiss, but she could only say, "Good night, Mr. James."

"Good night, Ms. Grand."

Heather did an about face and headed toward her room. Her nerves were in shock. She knew he stood there watching her walk away, but she dared not look back. Inside the room, she closed the door. She slid down to the floor to catch her breath. It was not what she expected from him. She expected him to have groupies lined up and ready to finish the party in their suite. This job was going to be harder than she thought, especially if he tried that again. She could not let that happen. She had to put her foot down. He could not jeopardize her career. She liked him as an artist and from afar, but she did not know what he was thinking kissing her like that. Heather stood up and gathered her composure. All of her luggage was already lined up in the room. A shower was the only thing she could think of that would make her feel better, so she thought.

That night in bed, Heather tossed and turned all night. The suite was quiet. No parties and no other voices. Just before dawn, Heather sat up in the bed, grabbed her laptop, and went into the kitchen. The wet bar faced the window that gave her an amazing view of the Las Vegas strip. The view also gave her some inspiration to write the article for the Vegas concert. Deep in thought, Heather did not hear Mark enter the room. He startled her by coming up behind her and leaning in to her ear, "I hope you're writing good things about me."

"Oh, shit! You scared me."

"I'm sorry. I just had to get you."

"You almost got it alright."

"Did you sleep alright?"

"No, not really."

"Why not. Was the bed not comfortable?"

"It wasn't that."

"Then what was it?"

"It's nothing. I think I just have to get used to being on the road."

"It takes some getting used to. We're leaving for

LA tonight. I have a meeting to attend for another project before we leave though."

"What project?"

"I am involved in non profit that advocates against childhood sexual abuse."

"Oh, I didn't realize that."

"It's something you can use, but I tend not to promote my philanthropy that much. It's personal."

"I understand."

Heather took that note and looked forward to tagging along to the meeting. The idea of telling Mark off about the kiss the night before, was a bust. She didn't have the nerve. The sound of her cellphone snapped her out of that thought. She ran to get it.

"Hi, Jus?"

"Hi! What's up!"

"I was going to call you today."

"Call me and tell me what? That you and Mark

B. are hitting it off?"

"What? Why would I say that?"

"Your pictures are all over social media."

"What? How?"

"You and Mark B. are a rumor on his opening tour night. This is awesome, girl!"

"No, it isn't. This is my job."

"Girl, you need to check out the media and him holding your hand in the crowd."

"Oh, that was not what it looked like."

"Ms. Grand, you are a journalist. You know it's hardly ever what it looks like. It is what the fans say it is."

"This is not how I thought this would go."

"Don't stress it. Do your job and let the rest play in the background. There will be rumors, so get over it."

"I don't know how long it will be a rumor."

"Excuse me?" Justice cleared her throat.

"He kissed me on the forehead last night before

bed."

"Wait a minute. A kiss before bed. Are you in the same hotel?"

"See, it's not how it looks. There was a problem with my hotel room so he invited me to stay here."

"Yeah, I bet there was a problem. He likes you, girl. You can't see that?"

"I don't know what I am seeing."

"I think you need to just let things happen. Don't go all militant on him. I know you. You like to stay so business minded and focused that you forget that men are human and need to see your gentle side sometime."

"I don't know how to do that anymore. I hung up my dating hat, so adding a celebrity to the list of failures is not the goal I had in mind."

"You're overthinking it. Just try."

Heather digressed. It was always a pointless debate to try and change what her best friend was thinking.

"What would I do without you?"

"I don't know," Justice teased. "Where are you off to next?"

"We are headed to LA tonight. The concert isn't for another two days, but I have this Vegas story to write and I can use the downtime."

"Darrin has a client to meet in LA in a couple days. I may fly out there with him. I need a mini vacay."

"That would be so nice. I'd love to see you."

"Do you want to come to the concert? I am sure I can get you tickets."

"You know I am not into rap."

"Come'on! Please. Do it for me."

"Alright, send me the details and tour schedule. I need to know where my sister is going to be at all times anyway."

"Yaaay. I can't wait."

"I have to get ready for an afternoon meeting, I know you're probably just getting up over there."

"Yes, I am. Talk to you later."

"Remember what I said, relax and let things just happen."

"I will try."

Heather stayed in the bedroom for a minute to think about what her best friend said. Unfortunately, of the good guys, Heather ran off every man that tried to be with her. She was so focused on getting her shot in the writing industry that she put it first before everything. She would cancel dates, be consumed by social media trying to keep up with the latest news, and would break up with men who tried to commit her to relationships too quickly.

"Breakfast in bed." Mark B. knocked as he rolled in a cart with a covered plate.

"You didn't have to…"

"I know. I wanted to. Please, enjoy. I'll bring your laptop."

"I was gonna…" Heather was talking to thin air.

Mark was already in route for the laptop and Heather just sat there looking at the breakfast tray.

"Here you go." Mark sat the laptop on the desk in the room.

"Thank you."

"This is as normal as life gets for me."

"What?" Heather raised an eyebrow.

"You know, this." Mark pointed at the tray of food.

"This what?"

"Being able to do things for someone like breakfast, getting your laptop, and just doing for someone else without hired help around."

"Oh. I see." Heather felt kind of sorry for him.

"I hope I didn't make you uncomfortable last night." Mark stood leaning in the doorway of the master bedroom.

"It was unexpected." She knew what he meant.

"But not uncomfortable."

"Right."

"That is good to know. Enjoy your breakfast. I am going to be in the gym for a while."

"Where is that?"

"It's on the other side of the living room, behind that partition."

"I may join you."

"That would be nice."

Mark turned and walk away. Heather could finally exhale after holding her breath looking at his already perfectly cut biceps and six pack abs.

Heather made sure to take her time with writing her article before taking a break. She had to make sure this article was one of her best. It would be the test of her talent. Her secret feelings for her muse had to be kept under control and that meant not allowing herself to sweat over his kindness. She had to ignore her best friend's suggestions to allow something to develop. That was a bad idea and she knew it.

In the gym, Mark was sweating profusely on the

treadmill. He wore his headphones, a brand he designed. Heather had always admired his savvy business portfolio. She had to remember to add that to her article.

"Glad you decided to join me." Mark removed an earbud from his ear.

"Yes, I better get it in now."

"Yeah, we'll be checking out in a couple hours. You don't have to attend my meeting. Feel free to go shopping or sight seeing."

"Oh, really. Thanks. I do need a few things."

Heather jumped on the elliptical machine next to Mark and started the machine at a comfortable pace. Mark was slowing down and went to the weights. After thirty minutes of pretending to be totally into her own workout, Heather hopped off the machine and headed back toward her room. She need a cold shower. She'd had enough.

"You're finished?" Mark asked before she turned the corner.

"Yeah, I just needed that jump start. I have to finish working on some things before we leave."

"Cool. I'll have someone from my team take you to wherever you need to go."

"Thanks, but I'll get a cab. I will meet you wherever you are."

Heather made an exit before he could insist. After her shower, Heather got dressed and was heading out. Mark was on the phone arguing with someone. He saw Heather and held up a finger gesturing for her to wait a minute. Heather stopped and took her purse off her shoulder. Mark was furious about something and it did not look good. He hung up the phone blaring obscenities.

"What is it?" Heather asked.

"It's my damn label."

"What happened?"

"I just had to fire Ms. Oni."

"Why?"

"She got herself in some hot water. Now they

want to send someone out here that I don't approve of to replace her."

"Well, what's wrong the replacement?"

"Me and Ms. Oni go way back. She can be in two places at one time and not miss a beat. I can't take a chance on some rookie out here. I want to hand pick my own PA."

"There are a lot of good PAs out there."

"Not like her."

"What are you going to do?"

"I have to think about it. I told them not to send anyone out here right now. Wait a minute…" Mark looked at Heather.

"Ooooh, no. Don't even think about it."

"You'd be perfect."

"No. I can't. I work for Musiq."

"I just need someone who can help with my social media sites, schedule meetings out on the tour and a few other things."

"Mark, I can't."

Mark came over to Heather and got down on one knee. "Please don't make me beg."

"Get up," she laughed, "No. I can't do it."

"Please." Mark was literally begging.

"I'll think about it." Heather gave in.

Mark stood up with a grin on his face that told Heather he was very pleased. "Thank you."

"Can I go shopping now?"

"Not without me."

"How? What about your meeting?"

"Well, I am free now. I also found out on my call that the meeting was cancelled. I have to reschedule."

"You. Go shopping? How?"

"Where there is a will, there is a way."

Mark popped a kiss on Heather's forehead and grabbed his cellphone, made a call and went into the other room. Seconds later, he had his baseball cap on, incognito shades and looked ready to go.

"Let's go."

"Okay." Heather let out a giggle at how excited Mark was about going to the mall. It felt kind of weird, but she was quickly adjusting to being around Mark like a friend. He definitely treated her like he wanted her around.

"What's so funny?" He asked.

"You."

"What?" He opened the door of the suite so they could walk out.

"You're excited about going to the mall."

"I get to go off script today. When a meeting is cancelled, I try to enjoy the moment."

"Where do you want to go?" Heather asked.

"To Caesars."

"That's where I was headed."

"Great minds think alike."

"That's what they say." Heather agreed.

When they reached the elevator, Mark's main security guard, Manny was inside when it opened.

"Ready, boss?"

"Let's do it."

"Hi, Ms. Grand." Manny said.

"Hi, Manny." Heather replied.

When they reached the lobby of the hotel, there was a light crowd. Mark grabbed Heather's hand and quickly exited to the car.

"You do know that people are going to think we're a couple." Heather said inside the car.

"People are going to talk."

"What does that mean?"

"It means, don't stress it. Most gossip isn't true."

"But a lot of it is." Heather was matter of fact.

Mark sat closer to Heather in the back of the extended cab SUV. He turned her face toward him and kissed her softly on the lips.

"I know." Mark said in agreement with Heather's statement.

Heather's heart probably stopped beating for a few seconds. He kissed her again and caressed her cheek.

"Mark, what are you doing?"

"I've wanted to do that since that day you put me in my place in that conference room."

Heather cleared her throat, "We can't do this, Mark."

"I knew you would say that."

"Then why would you do that. We're supposed to be working together." Heather explained.

"I knew you would say that, too."

"I mean, you seem like a nice guy, but I don't know you."

"I'm just a nice guy, huh?"

"Look, I don't do celebrities. Is that better?"

"You don't do celebrities, wow."

Heather didn't have a comeback for that. It did sound bad the way it came out, but she had to let him know that it was not going to go down like that.

"I'll respect that." Mark said and moved back over to the other side of the SUV.

"I appreciate it."

When they arrived at Caesar's hotel, Mark did not treat Heather any different because of her statement. He was very generous and made sure that he knew where she was at all times. He insisted on paying for whatever she wanted. He watched her more than the security detail seemed to watch him. He did respectfully keep his distance and she made a mental note about that change in his demeanor.

When they entered a designer store Heather heard a girl shout, "Mark B."

Manny went out to the fan and talked to her. He motioned for Mark to come over to them. Mark looked back for Heather who waved him off to go ahead without her, but he had no intentions on leaving her behind. He grabbed her hand and brought her over to the fan who wanted an autograph and picture.

"I'll take the picture." Heather offered.

The fan obliged and stood next to Mark and hugged him closely. After the photo Mark took the time to write out her autograph and before he could finish, a crowd had formed. Heather was falling further and further behind the crowd. Not a minute passed before Mark and Manny broke through the crowd and grabbed Heather and pulled her toward the nearest exit.

"You have to stay close to me." Mark scolded.

"I was." Heather said pathetically.

"I mean close. I have to know where you are and when I didn't see you anymore I got nervous."

"You don't have to babysit me, Mark."

"It's not about that. Because you'll be with me for the next few months, people will see you with me and try to get to me through you."

"Oh. I didn't realize that."

"Yea, so it's not about me trying to babysit you. It's about your safety."

"I'm sorry."

Mark scolded Manny too for allowing the crowd to close him in that way. Heather felt like a little girl who lost her parent in the mall. When they reached the exit, Manny went out to make sure the SUV was ready to go. A small crowd followed closely behind them the entire walk back to the car.

"A taste of my normal." Mark smiled.

Inside the car, Heather smiled, but did not respond thinking about his normal. She did not know what to say or feel. She definitely did not want this to blow up in her face. On the ride, Heather reminisced about her past experiences.

First there was Willie.

Willie was a native New Yorker she met in college. They dated for a year. He was miserable in college. He was only there because his parents wanted him to be a doctor, but he had no ambition. He was chasing their dream and spent so much time drinking that he failed and dropped out of school.

Then there was Nathan.

Nathan was the white collar psycho. They met through a mutual friend. He was all about the Benjamins. So much so that he wanted Heather to do business under the table to make money. He thought she was wasting time in college and of course he didn't go. He made money hustling and scheming people out of theirs. That didn't last three months.

Then there was Phillip.

Phillip was the NBA reject who did not want to do anything except play ball. When he was cut from the team, he lost all of his motivation for their relationship. He thought he was too good to work a regular job, so he started messing around with other women who had money. Heather all of a sudden was just not his type.

Finally, there was Winston.

Winston was the most promising guy who turned out to be secretly bisexual. In a candid conversation about sexual fantasies, he revealed that he had sex with a man and enjoyed it. Heather respectfully ended that relationship before they ever had sex.

Due to one crazy experience after another, Heather had put dating on hold. Since she started her career as a hip hop journalist she hasn't dated anyone and a celebrity was definitely not on the list. She had been writing for hip hop columns since college and the women were relentless. She already knew what it was like being a groupie because some of those fans made the best stories. Remarkably, Mark seemed to have a good team and the women were usually one step behind him. Not every celebrity was receiving bad press with the ladies and Mark B. James was one of them.

Heather's phone rang interrupting her thoughts. She peeked at the caller ID. It was Justice.

"Hey."

"You two look so cute together." She said.

"What are you talking about?"

"Girl, you are a journalist and you have not been watching social media."

"I have been trying to capture details for my story. What did you see?"

"You two in the mall at Caesar's Mall. It's all over iGram."

"Pull up iGram." Heather said to Mark.

He looked at her awkwardly, but pulled out his phone and opened the app. He looked and smiled.

"What?" Heather was asking Mark.

"What did he do?" Justice asked.

"He is smiling." Heather said gesturing for Mark to pass the phone.

"He likes you, Heather."

"I know that, Justice." Heather wasn't smiling as she looked at the picture.

"Why do you sound so upset about it. You have dreamed of being this close to Mark B. James since we were in college."

"I know, but it's different now."

"How? Why?"

"Because, it just is." Heather said looking at Mark who was listening to the conversation. Heather gave Mark back his phone and turned her head to look out of the window.

"Justice, I'll talk to you later."

"Fine."

"We'll talk in LA. See you tomorrow, chica."

"Bye."

Heather ended the call as they were pulling up to the hanger where the jet was parked.

"We're headed out? I didn't get my bags from the hotel."

"Heather, you don't have to worry about your things. We have everything taken care of. Relax, sweetie."

"I'm trying to adjust. This is not my lifestyle. I am used to doing things for myself." She tried to open the door, but it was locked. She sighed in frustration.

Mark chuckled, "Let me get that for you." He exited the car and came around and opened the door.

"Thank you." She said.

"As long as you're with me, you'll never touch another door again. Is that clear?"

"Never?" She asked.

"Never."

"I'm clear."

Heather smiled inside at his gentleman-like gesture. That earned him a few cool points for opening her door, but she was not ready for everything else.

CHAPTER FOUR

The LA concert was wilder than any Heather had ever seen. The coliseum was so loud Heather could not stand stage side. She sat completely backstage and watched from the production room. By the end of the concert, she made her way back out stage side to capture the last few fan reactions to the finale.

Mark came running off the stage and nearly ran into Heather. "Hey, baby!"

"Hi." Heather replied before she could catch herself.

Mark went over to the refreshment station and took a bottle of water from it and ran back out on stage. The rest of his crew were still hyping the crowd. They did one more song before the lights went dim and the show was over.

"This way Ms. Grand." Manny came up to Heather escorting her away from the stage.

"Where are we going?"

"To the after party. Last time, I got my ass chewed out for not taking care of you so, I will come back for Mark after I take you."

Heather followed Manny to another part of the coliseum where the party was. When inside, the first person she saw was Justice.

"Hi!" She ran over to her best friend and embraced her.

"Hey!" Their embrace rocked back and forth as they smiled.

"Did you enjoy the show?" Heather asked.

"Of course. We watched it from here. You

know I am more about networking."

"Right."

"Where's Mark?" Justice asked.

"He's coming in a minute, I guess." Heather said looking back at the door.

"So, you know there is already rumors that you and Mark are seeing each other."

Heather rolled her eyes, "How do these stories start so fast?"

"Duh! You're a writer. You know how they start."

"It's just never happened to me before so it's not fair." Heather pouted.

"Not fair!" Justice laughed out loud.

"What's so funny?"

"You!"

"You're acting like you don't like Mark or something."

"I do, but I don't want to. Not like that. Not now."

"Well, get over that. He likes you."

"How do you know?"

A waitress walked up and offered the ladies a cocktail.

"I found out that he is a client of Darrin's colleague."

"He specifically requested you for this job. That is why they called you back after a month."

"What? How? He doesn't even know me."

"They selected someone else and he told them, no. Darrin mentioned you to his colleague and that is how he looked you up. It got to the point where he was going to pull out of the deal if Musiq couldn't get you to accept their offer."

"Wow. So, I got this job because he likes me?"

"No, silly! He likes your work, and he likes you."

"This is sounding worse by the minute." Heather took a long swig of her cocktail, then motioned for the waitress to bring over another.

"Hi, Ms. Grand." Darrin walked up to greet the

ladies.

"Hi. Glad you two could make it." Heather greeted.

"Well, I had business and you know Justice, she loves to shop on Rodeo Drive so here we are."

"There you are." Mark walked up to them and hugged Heather.

"Hi Darrin and if it isn't the infamous Justice Swank." Mark said.

"You know them?" Heather asked.

"Yes, I have seen the second most beautiful face in New York on television," he leaned over and kissed Justice on the cheek. "And Darrin and I go way back." Mark winked.

"It is a pleasure to finally meet you in person." Justice said.

"Thank you for coming. Have some drinks and party a little bit. I am trying to loosen up your girl, here. She is always in work mode."

"I'll get her right while I'm here." Justice teased.

"Please and excuse me, I have someone I have to talk to," Mark smiled. He whispered in Heather's ear before walking away. She smiled and Justice looked intrigued.

"That's my queue, babe." Darrin kissed Justice on the cheek and walked away.

"What was that about?" Justice couldn't hold it.

"He told me not to drink too many of these." Heather held up the glass.

"He's so fresh." Justice laughed.

Heather gulped down the drink and summoned the waitress for another. The girls started to mingle with the party. They danced and had a great time. It had been a while. They worked different hours and found little time when they could go out and enjoy the city life. Mark had apparently changed clothes for the party because he wore a nicely fitted t-shirt to accentuate his physique. Heather caught Mark watching her a few times, and she pretended not to notice the model groupies gawking over him.

By the end of the night, Heather had had too many drinks, but she was having such a good time she did not seem to care.

"Heather, it's time to go." Mark came over to the VIP section where she was sitting.

"Already?" Heather sounded disappointed.

"We have an early flight tomorrow." Mark explained as he walked over to a few other people and gave them handshakes and dap.

"Duty calls." Heather slurred and sat her drink on the table and stood up.

"I guess we'll have to go shopping next time." Justice said hugging her friend good-bye.

"I guess so." Heather frowned.

Justice whispered during their hug, "Have fun with this, Heather. Be open to whatever happens."

"I'm scared to."

"Fear nothing." Justice said.

Mark returned and grabbed Heather by the hand and led her toward the door. She turned back to look at her friend who was watching them walk away. Justice blew a kiss in their direction. Heather winked and walked out of the party.

At the hotel suite, Heather did not ask why she did not have her own suite. She just went to the room that she knew would be hers. Once inside, she flopped on the bed. The room started spinning and she couldn't move. The fruity cocktails were taking their toll. Mark tapped on the door.

"Are you alright?"

"Huh?" Heather mumbled.

Mark came over to the bed and got on his knee and was level with Heather laying on the bed. He just stared at her.

"What do you like about me?" Heather managed to say.

"Hmmm. I think I will tell you that when you're not intoxicated, because I want you to remember what I say."

"What can you tell me right now?" Heather

asked with a drunkard's slow speech.

"You don't act like all of the others." Mark said as he caressed the baby hairs that were sweaty on her forehead.

"What others?" Heather was surprisingly following the conversation.

"Other women who are around me."

"How do they act?"

"Like a fan or a groupie."

"I am a fan."

"I wouldn't know it. You treat me like a client."

"You are a client." Heather slurred.

Mark giggled. "I know, and I respect that you have maintained that boundary."

"Why haven't you?" Heather was curious.

"I'm a man. I like what I like and want what I want."

"Ohhh, my." Heather's face cringed.

"What? Did I say something wrong?"

"My stomach."

"Do you have to…"

Before he could get it out, Heather sat up and threw up all over the bed. "I'm so sorry."

"It's okay, sweetie. They'll clean it up."

"Come on, let's get you cleaned up."

"I can do it." Heather said getting undressed while Mark was still in the room.

"Okay, well I'll be in the other room. Let me know if you need anything." He seemed to rush out of the room before Heather finished undressing.

Heather was embarrassed and just wanted to be alone. The shower helped calm her. When she came out of the room, the sheets were pulled from the bed. She went to the kitchen and found Mark sitting at the wet bar.

"Thank you."

"For what?"

"You know." Heather motioned to the bedroom.

"Oh, that." Mark smiled as he scrolled through his phone.

"What are you looking at?" She asked sheepishly.

Heather had secured the over sized white robe from the bathroom. She closed it tightly and looked over his shoulder. In that moment, she looked at the back of his neck and smelled the scent from his cologne. It was memorizing. She put her arm on his shoulder and leaned in to read his phone.

"It was the news report about the concert tonight. The local news did a good piece on it and look there's you on iGram again."

"Oh, boy. People are going to say whatever they want, true or not."

Mark turned in the stool and Heather was now between his legs. He grabbed her by the waist and pulled her closer to him. Heather leaned into him. He kissed her deeply. They tongue played long enough for Mark to untie Heather's robe. It opened and revealed her light mocha skin, perky breast and cleanly shaven pussy.

"Wow." Mark said as he kissed her breasts that sat up so firmly in front of his face. He leaned in, hugged her body tightly, and inhaled her energy, then he exhaled it. Heather wrapped her arms around his neck and laid her chin on the top of his head. She closed her eyes in disbelief. Mark B. was in her arms...how could this be?

"Let's go lay down." Mark said picking Heather up and carrying her to his master bedroom. Heather wasn't prepared for this part. What would she do? She thought of resisting, but she didn't. Instead she let him take her. She laid her head on his chest as he carried her. He sat her on the bed, then he grabbed a t-shirt from his bag and helped Heather out of her robe and into it. He pulled back the comforter, helped her into bed, and he went into the bathroom. By the time he finished his shower, Heather was asleep.

When she finally turned during the night, she found Mark asleep on his side of the bed. She scooted over to be closer to him. He stirred when he felt her. He turned over and let her lay on his chest. He tickled her forehead with his fingers, "You okay?"

"I am now." Heather snuggled closer and went back to sleep.

By morning, Mark was kissing her all over her body. It woke her up and when she realized where he was kissing, her body was already responding.

"Morning." He said in the middle of kissing her thigh.

"Hi." Heather was groggy.

"I want you."

"I want you." Heather confessed.

"Then I guess we should give each other what we want."

Heather smiled as she looked down at Mark ready to kiss her warm sweet spot. Mark took full control and gave Heather a morning she'd never forget. Mark seductively kissed her entire body, giving her chills. Soft moans escaped her mouth when he finally sucked on her sweet spot. Gently and with confidence he licked and played with her until she exploded all over his lips. He teased her more and more. She came again and again. After countless orgasms, she swiftly clasped her legs closed to catch her breath. She exhaled and panted loudly to catch her breath, but Mark spread her legs again and sat up on his knees to show his well endowed erection. He scooted her closer, grabbing her hips, then he popped a condom package, and entered her with ease. He moaned with each stroke into her wetness.

"Open your eyes, baby." Mark whispered.

Heather opened her eyes to find him watching her closely and deeply. She was lost in the moment. She felt his strokes go deeper and deeper until his moan matched her. Her hips moved with the rotation of his stride, they fit together like hand and glove. Out of practice, Heather allowed Mark to guide her as he delved deeper and consistently until they reached their peak together.

The rumor was actually true. Heather recalled from some industry gossip about Mark B. James. It was the best she'd ever had.

After their morning session, Mark ordered room service and then they prepared for their flight. On the way to the hanger, Heather received a call.

"This is Heather."

"Hi Ms. Grand, this is Ms. Innis."

"Hi."

"We need to talk about the project?"

"What about it? My article is not due for another couple days."

"It's not about the article."

"Then what is it about?" Heather looked at Mark who sat close enough to hear both sides of the conversation.

"It's about you and Mark. The tabloids are catching pictures of you and him a little too close. You are there to do a job, Ms. Grand."

"I know what my job is and what you will see in the tabloids is to be expected."

"What do you mean to be expected?"

"We are spending a lot of time together. So there will be photos of us."

"Is there something going on between you and Mark?" Ms. Innis asked bluntly.

"Excuse me?" Heather was appalled.

"Is everything okay?" Mark interrupted.

Heather looked at Mark with a death stare.

"Ms. Innis, I will have this talk with you in the office. I will be back in New York next week."

"Is that Mark?" Ms. Innis asked.

"Good-bye Ms. Innis." Heather ignored her boss's inquiry and hung up the phone. "This is exactly what I wanted to avoid." Heather stuffed her phone in her purse.

"What exactly are you trying to avoid?"

"Drama."

"So I am drama, now?"

"I did not mean it like that."

"Well, it sure as hell sounded like it."

"I am a very private person. I have done well keeping out of the industry drama and relationships. All they are doing is being nosy. I mean, what did they expect would happen with us spending so much time together?"

"Heather, please relax. What are they going to do, fire you?"

"Maybe."

"They can't. I have to hip you to the game on this side of the business. They need this to work to sell their silly ass magazines to people who like reading that shit. Besides, I have a say in this and you ain't going nowhere."

"So what are you saying?" Heather was not following.

"Just go there and meet with them and tell them to stay the fuck out of your personal life. What you and I do have nothing to do with your writing ability, right?"

"True."

"Then don't let them push you away from me. We're just getting started."

"Oh, are we?"

"Yes and you'll enjoy every minute of it."

Mark grabbed Heather and brought her into his embrace. He tickled her side and she squealed and laughed hard like a little kid.

"Stop!" Heather pleaded.

Mark got one more tickle in before he cradled her in his arms in the back of the SUV and kissed her gently on the lips.

"Now, you better write a bomb ass story or your ass will be fired."

"I know right!" Heather laughed.

As Heather walked through the hallway of Musiq, everyone looked her way. It was like a scene from a movie. The whispers, snickers, and pointing as she walked to her office. Heather held her head high and did not flinch. She had nothing to prove and nothing to confirm. She and Mark had agreed to keep it out of the airwaves and let people speculate as they would do anyway.

Not a minute passed before Ms. Innis was at the door tapping. "Knock, knock."

"Come in."

"First, I have to tell you that your piece on Mark B. is amazing. The editors are very pleased and cannot wait to get that issue on the shelves." Ms. Innis said taking the vacant seat in front of Heather's desk.

"Thank you. It has been quite an adjustment."

"I can imagine."

"That brings me to my concerns about you and the photos circulating on iGram."

"What about them?"

"What is the story behind them?"

"I was quite concerned at first, but Mark B. had to school me on how this was going to work."

"How so?" Ms. Innis leaned in closer.

"He said that I am his shadow. That meant I'd be where he is at all times. It was quite an adjustment as I stated. I did not like it and I definitely did not want to be the topic of gossip."

"Well, it's too late for that. The word is you two are an item."

"An item?" Heather giggled.

"Well, it does look like he holds you a little close in the photos."

"Nothing is compromising and in fact, being this close is how I will be able to write these columns."

"I heard Ms. Oni was let go." Ms. Innis said.

"Yes, I was told that she was no longer working

for Retrospect."

"I heard that Mark had …" Ms. Innis started.

"Look, Ms. Innis, this is not the reason I am here. I came to the office to clear up things with your inquiry and make sure my column was ready for print. I don't know any details about Ms. Oni." Heather stated firmly.

Ms. Innis was offended by the interruption and stood up abruptly, "Well, don't get your ass fired is all I was about to say."

"I am far from being fired. I am doing the job I was hired to do. What I do in my personal time is not up for discussion and I hope that we won't need to have this conversation again."

"I hope not. Just know that I've warned you." Ms. Innis said before she left the office.

Heather seemed confused and frustrated with Ms. Innis' last statement. What was she warning her about and what happened to Ms. Oni? Did she know everything involved in that situation? What was Mark not telling her?

"Justice." Heather said excitedly over the phone.

"Hey! Where are you?"

"I'm in New York. Do you have a minute?"

"Yea, what's up?"

"Let's meet up for lunch."

"Sure. Our favorite spot?"

"Yep."

"See you in an hour."

Heather had to talk to her bestie. Things were starting to get messy and Heather needed to find out if she was getting herself into something she'd regret. Musiq was obviously privy to some information that Heather didn't know about and it would behoove her to find out before something blew up in her face.

Heather took the subway to midtown to their

favorite sandwich spot, Sal's. The ride was a lot different than the plush vehicles that she had been riding around in lately. It actually felt a little grimy and dirty. When she got off and walked up to the street, she thought about that life of luxury that Mark lived. It was his normal to be in nice, clean, and fancy places and this used to be hers, nasty subways, smelly taxis, and homeless hustlers on every corner begging for change. Did her and Mark really fit? Was she in over her head, she thought.

At the table of the sandwich shop, she could see her friend Justice getting out of a limo. Heather smiled and shook her had at her friend who lived that life because of her fancy boyfriend. Heather waved her hand in the air to get her attention.

"Hey, sis." Heather stood to greet her friend.

"You sounded like something was wrong. What is it?"

"It's Mark." Heather sat first.

"What about him? What did he do?"

"Nothing. He's been perfect."

"Then what the hell is it?" Justice finally sat down.

"Musiq called me in for a meeting about the pictures on iGram. They suspect something is going on between Mark and me."

"Well, it isn't. You said you wouldn't do anything with him so what are they worried about?" Justice said matter of fact.

Heather looked sheepishly down at the table, almost embarrassed to look at her friend.

"Well there isn't, is there?"

"We crossed the line over a week ago."

"A week!" Justice leaned in and yelled in a whisper.

"Yeah."

"And you're just now telling me this. Girl, that is great. I mean this is your dream. You should be happy."

"I am, but my job is all in my business."

"So what!"

"Did you spit out a banging ass piece to the editor?"

"Of course."

"Then that's all they need to be concerned about."

"I just feel like I am sleeping with my client."

"Girl, stop being so professional. You have been in love with Mark B. James since he dropped his first album, "Love & Money". You are living a dream right now. I am so happy for you."

"There's something else."

"What?"

"His old personal assistant, Ms. Oni. I need you to find out why she got fired."

"Why?"

"It's just something my boss said and I don't want anything to backfire or come out and I don't know about it."

Justice was already dialing on her phone in the

middle of Heather completing her reason.

"Yes, babe. I need you to find out something for me. The PA for Mark B. James…yea, her. Tell me why she was let go. Call me back, pronto. K, babe…bye."

"Jus, you didn't have to find out now."

"Why not. He'll get us that information before we finish lunch. Let's order, I'm starved and I want to hear about this last week you've had."

Heather smiled and giggled giving her friend a high-five. It had been a while since Heather was able to share any juice from her love life. Justice listened to the story and beamed with pride as she watched Heather's glow. Their lunch was like old college times. There was always some guy to talk about in between homework and projects. By the time they finished lunch, and just as Justice had predicted, her phone rang.

"Yeah, babe. Uh, huh. Yea, okay. That's it. Okay, thanks babe. Call you about dinner plans later. Bye."

Heather looked anxiously at her friend, "Well?"

"Apparently, Ms. Oni did not like the new arrangement with you joining their team on the tour."

"What? That is ridiculous. Why would she not like that?"

"The rumor is she had a thing for Mark, but he never took her up on it. And when she found out that you were going to be attached at the hip to him, she asked for another journalist. When Mark B. said, no, she threatened to quit so he fired her."

"Mark never told me the reason and Ms. Innis made it sound like there was more to it than that. Are you sure Darrin has the whole story?"

"He is the best we can get without you asking Mark about the chick yourself."

"I am not going to do that. She is gone and I don't have anything to do with why she got fired."

"Well, not personally, but she blames you, I'm

sure."

"A bitter woman is not my cup of tea." Heather rolled her eyes.

"So, sounds like you need to talk to Mark and find out if there is anything you need to worry about."

"I will."

"Well, chica, I have to get back to the station. I have some paperwork to get in before I leave. I can't wait to read this column you wrote."

"It'll be out next week."

"Kisses." Justice kissed her friend on the cheek and started out the door. Heather sat and scrolled through her phone to see the latest on iGram. Here eyes bugged out when she saw a picture of Mark wrapped up with another woman. The picture was tagged just an hour ago. Heather was furious. She dialed Mark's number immediately.

"Hi."

"Hi, babe." Mark answered with a smile in his

voice.

"Where are you?" Heather asked.

"In the city. Where are you?" Mark asked.

"I'm in midtown at Sal's Deli."

"I love that spot. I'm coming over there right now."

"No, I was just leaving."

"Don't go. I'm coming to pick you up. I will text you exactly what I want on my sandwich." Mark hung up before Heather could say no. She didn't want to order a sandwich. She wanted to know who was the woman in the photo. The anger boiled even higher as she waited in line for the sandwich. By the time she checked out, a black extended SUV was parked out front. Mark came inside like he owned the place. The patrons all stared as he walked toward Heather.

"Hi, Sal!" Mark yelled to the owner of the deli.

"B!" Sal answered as he came from behind the counter to give Mark a fist bump.

"You know I had to come in for my favorite sandwich."

"Yeah, when Heather here ordered it, I was wondering who it was for. She's been one of my regulars since she was a freshman in college. I didn't know you two were friends."

"We work together." Heather interjected.

"Yea, we work together." Mark confirmed.

The patrons watched the exchange and did not stop eating and none of them asked for Mark's autograph. Mark paid for the sandwich and said his goodbyes to Sal. Outside the shop, Mark put Heather's arm in his and escorted her inside the truck.

"Thanks." Mark took the sandwich from the bag and bit into it like he hadn't eaten in days.

"You're welcome." Heather said watching him eat.

"Are you okay?" Mark asked sensing a little tension.

"I know this is going to sound so cliché, but who is this woman in the picture?"

"What picture?" Mark stopped eating.

"This picture." Heather showed him the picture.

"She's a fan. I was just at a benefit around the corner and she was the organizer."

"It just looked like something else."

"Baby, it's going to look like that a lot. You know people will be in photos with me a lot. You can't be concerned about that. It's part of my normal remember—we talked about my normal."

"I have to get used to it. I am not a jealous person, but I can be possessive."

"You can be all the possessive you need. Just always ask me about things before jumping to conclusions."

"That's fair. One more thing, while we're on the subject."

"Shoot."

"What was the reason Ms. Oni was fired."

Mark stopped eating and this time he put his sandwich down. He sighed and hesitated before he answered.

"It was because of you."

"Me? Why?"

"She wanted to replace you. I think she saw how I looked at you that day in the conference room and it made her jealous. She had tried to push up on me before, but she's just not my type. I rejected her and since then she'd been a little bitter, but she still did her damn job."

"Is there anything else about her that I should know?"

"Other than the fact that she and your boss Daniel have had a thing that she thinks no one knows about, no."

"Ewww, really?" Heather said in disbelief.

"She's the reason we started this tour deal with Musiq, but unfortunately, when the deal was inked, she was no longer in control. I interviewed a few people, but I wasn't feeling any of them. I got the referral from a mutual friend and that is how I found you. Musiq and Retrospect were already bought in. Ms. Oni became a liability when she tried to tell me who I could have on my tour."

"Then why didn't you want a replacement for her?" Heather inquired.

"I really can't stomach a new PA right now. I am in the middle of a tour and I don't have time to train or bring someone new up to speed." Mark explained.

Heather scooted closer to Mark and wiped the corner of his mouth, then she kissed his cheek. "I don't like mayonnaise." Heather tried to change the subject.

"I take it we're good." Mark wasn't ready to change it just yet.

"Yes, I am satisfied. I just want to stay in the know if we're going to do this. Secrets or half ass stories are not going to fly. If you can trust me enough to be with you, then you have to trust me with anything that could potentially come back and bite me in the ass."

Mark chuckled. "Fair enough. I have not had a lot of experience with relationships since I became a...you know...celebrity, so we're both going to learn how to do this together."

"Deal." Heather held out her pinky finger and Mark locked his with hers. He kissed her hand to seal the deal.

♠♠♠

The next stop was Toronto. On the jet, Heather made her way to the suite for a nap with Mark on her heels. It was hard to keep Mark away from her now. Somehow they made time for sex at 35,000 feet in the air.

Heather faced Mark after an explosive orgasm, "I am not drunk now." Heather said randomly.

"I know." Mark was confused.

"You never told me what you see in me."

"Oh, yeah. That was so long ago. How about I show you?"

"How do you plan to do that?"

Mark kissed her nipples that were standing so perfecting at attention. Heather was tickled by the sensation. Mark crawled near her perfect part, and licked her softly and seductively. Heather moaned and pinched her nipples which stimulated her even more. Mark was a genius at his clit game. "Ooooh, ahhhhh!" Heather knew a gush of cum was on its way. "Yessss!"

"Hmmmm, yeah, I like to hear that." Mark kissed her clit over and over and caused another gush to splash all over the bed.

"Ahhhh! Hmmmm." Heather softly moaned as she caught her breath.

"Do I still have to tell you?" Mark asked.

"Yes." Heather insisted.

"I am glad we have hours before we get to our destination."

"Me, too."

And as soon as their heated moment of passion was head for overtime, they were interrupted by a tap on the door. "Who the hell?" Mark grunted and put on his boxers.

He opened the door and stepped out. He came back after a few minutes and started to put his clothes on.

"What is it?"

"I have to get on a conference call about the concert in Toronto."

"Is everything alright?"

"Yea, just shit that Oni would handle and I got to do it. See if you took the job, I'd be able to send you in there to handle it." Mark joked.

"Yea, about that. Things are complicated now."

"Yea, I know. I can't have you working for me and working me at the same time." Mark laughed.

"Exactly." Heather smiled.

"Actually, you'd have the best of both worlds."

"How so?" Heather confused.

"I'd do everything you say, in the boardroom and the bedroom."

"I never thought of it that way. Maybe I should reconsider." Heather smiled.

"Oh, no. It's too late." Mark laughed as he zipped up his pants.

Heather tossed a pillow at Mark as he pulled his shirt over his head.

"I'm gonna get you for that." Mark promised as he disappeared behind the door to the main cabin.

Heather flopped back down on the plush bed and closed her eyes. She was living a dream.

They flew from city to city and from country to county. Heather was living two different lives, one as a journalist and the other secretly as Mark's woman. Wherever they went, Mark and Heather made sure to smile for the cameras. The hip hop column of Musiq became the talk of the industry. People wanted to know if they were an item, if they were getting married, and if Heather was pregnant. The gossip was endless, but Heather kept all of their gossip out of the column.

CHAPTER FIVE

A few months into the tour, Heather knew she'd get a little break to do some ground work. Back in Heather's hometown of Atlanta for the Entertainment Television Awards, Musiq Magazine was one of the major media platforms covering the event. Heather was asked to co-host the Red Carpet with Flosia Reynolds. Flosia was a fashion guru who craved the Red Carpet festivities. Heather was not so excited, but since her column was such a hit, they wanted to put a face to the column for the cameras. This was not what she had in mind for this event, but she went along with the plan to make her bosses happy.

"Who are you wearing?" Flosia asked Heather as they were getting their mics ready for the event.

"Excuse me?" Heather was not prepared to answer.

"What designer are you wearing tonight?" Flosia looked annoyed.

"I am not being interviewed, so that's not important."

"Oh, but it is."

"Look, I am not a fan of this gig, so let's just do the interviews and be done with it." Heather was matter of fact.

"Well, excuse me."

"Now that we have that straight, I will be back when it's time to start the set." Heather walked off.

"Wait…where are you going?" Flosia yelled.

Heather did not answer. She pretended not to

hear her and kept walking toward the media dressing room. Inside was a lot of dressing and make up going on for those who were part of the event. The whispers and looks started as soon as Heather passed a few women sitting in front of the mirror.

"Is there a problem?" Heather stopped and said confidently.

The two women hissed, but they turned their heads the other way.

"I didn't think so." Heather rolled her eyes and kept walking to her make-up station.

Heather thought that the night would be interesting, but now she knew it would definitely leave a memorable mark. She hoped that she didn't need to put anyone else in their place. The thing she feared was unraveling before here eyes. Her privacy was being invaded and the little bit of romance she was starting to experience was becoming public gossip. There was nothing she could do about that now. The show was about to begin and Heather had to get her mind right to deal with the crowd and her annoying co-host.

On the red carpet, Heather did banging interviews with the hottest artists in the industry. Mark B. arrived and Flosia was all over him during the interview. Heather had a hint of jealousy, but after his interview with Flosia, Mark came over to Heather and whispered in her hear, "I can't wait to make love to you tonight." Heather blushed and nodded in agreement.

"Flosia and Ms. Grand, it was a pleasure." Mark said and exited the red carpet.

"It was nice to finally meet you." Flosia's face glittered with a smile.

"You are such a groupie." Heather blurted.

"Excuse you!" Flosia turned her neck around really fast.

"You are not supposed to flirt with the artists. You are supposed to fit in with them. You are not just a reporter. You work for the hottest magazine on the shelf. Act like it."

"Well damn. Thanks, but no thanks for the advice." Flosia flipped her weave over her shoulder and smiled at the next guest approaching the red carpet.

"Suit yourself." Heather said.

"I will. I know exactly what am doing." Flosia started the interview with a young hip hop artist.

By the end of the red carpet show, Heather's feet were on fire. High heels were not her thing. As soon as she reached the dressing room, she stepped out of them. As Heather was reaching down to unhook her shoe, Flosia came bursting in the dressing room.

"Where is that bitch?!" Flosia yelled as she came storming down the hall.

"Who are you talking about?" Mandy stood up and questioned.

"That bitch, Heather." Flosia said as she reached

Heather's dressing vanity.

"Why are you yelling?" Heather said from her seat.

"You need to fire this hoe." Flosia said pointing her finger in Heather's face.

"Hoe? I was not the one flaunting over all the celebs on the red carpet."

"Just because you are fucking Mark B. don't excuse your ass from flaunting all over the celebs."

"Excuse me?" Heather stood up and faced Flosia.

"Ladies!" Mandy came over to stand between them.

"Your dumb ass don't even know who you're dealing with. He fucks all of his female employees." Flosia yelled.

The stares of onlookers were noticeable in the background. Heather was trapped in a venom of drama.

"You don't know what you're talking about and

to be clear, I don't *work* for Mark B, idiot." Heather said as she slipped into her comfortable flat shoes and gathered her heels. "This is so not my scene."

"Yes, Heather. Go." Mandy agreed.

"Don't worry, I am. By the way, I am going back to my hotel. My job is done here." Heather said and strutted out of the dressing room with her head held high. Mandy and Flosia looked at each other and shook their heads.

On the other side of the door, Heather briefly closed her eyes and took a deep breath in relief that she did not lose her cool over Flosia's comment. Mark was turning the corner and ran into Heather as she stood there with her eyes closed.

"Is everything alright, babe?" He asked concerned.

"It will be as soon as I get out of here." Heather said.

"Wait. What happened?"

"Let's talk about it later. I don't want to ruin

your night."

"Ruin my night?" Mark was confused.

"I'll see you back at the hotel." Heather said.

"Wait…you aren't going to stay and watch my nomination."

"I'm sorry. I have to get out of here." Heather said and left Mark standing there watching her walk away.

When she reached the curb, Heather hailed a cab. When she got inside, she felt so humiliated that she yelled an obscenity out loud, "Got dammit!"

"Are you okay, miss?" The cab driver asked looking through the rearview.

"I'm fine. Take me to 50 Jackson Avenue in Buckhead."

"Yes, ma'am."

Heather knew there was something more between Ms. Oni and Mark. He lied about it and the reason she was fired. Heather had to get the real truth and only Mark could tell her.

When Heather arrived at her parent's estate, there seemed to be a house full of guests. It was the last thing she expected, but it was too late. The cab was pulling off for his next fare. When inside, Heather tried to slip through the crowd, but her mother saw her.

"Heather!" Helen said.

"Hi, mom." Heather barely spoke as she kept walking toward her room.

"Wait. What are you doing here? I thought you were working the event? I saw your live Red Carpet Show. You looked stunning sweetheart."

"I was, but my gig was over so I slipped out. I just want to go to my room and get some quiet time. I'm sorry I interrupted your party." Heather said.

"Are you alright, honey?" Her mother knew something was wrong.

"I will be fine."

"Alright, let me know if you need anything. I'll keep everyone out of your hair."

"Thanks, mom."

Heather made her way to her room that still had all of her furniture in it. It was far enough from the main house that she could not hear any of the shenanigans. She looked at her bed and fell flat faced on it and screamed inside her pillow. She beat the bed with her fists to let out more frustration. "How could I be so stupid?" She said out loud. Tears began to form and the anger turned to disappointment. Heather knew she couldn't continue with Mark B. She had to end it before she really got hurt.

The tears dried up and Heather fell asleep. A tap on the door woke her up, "Heather, honey." Her father, Michael whispered.

"Hmmm, hi daddy."

"Sweetheart, Mr. James is here to see you."

"What?"

"He told me that he was here to pick you up for your flight."

"Okay. I'll be out in a minute."

"He's waiting on your terrace out back. Is everything OK, honey? Is he treating you, right?"

"How do you know?" Heather asked.

"You're here and weren't there supporting him on his big night. I keep up with my baby girl, you know. I see that twinkle in your eye. I know you're in love with him." Her father said.

"Daddy, I'm just so bad with relationships and picking good guys." Heather tried to explain.

"Well, sweetheart, I remember when I met your mother. She was young, pretty, smarter than me, and very hard to get. She wouldn't let me date her until I knew her for at least three months. She made us start a friendship and the rest blossomed from there. You set the tone, but you have to be consistent with what your boundaries are. If he wants to be with you, then he has to earn it."

"Thanks, Daddy. I never knew mom made you court her." Heather teased.

"So you know what that is, huh? Men forget about that sometime and want to just jump right in. It's up to the women to set the pace for how fast or slow it's going to go."

"Well, I guess I better go out there and face him."

"Yes, I think so. Come here darling." Her father said.

Heather huffed and sat up on the bed. Her father gave her the hug that she needed to get up and go face Mark. She went to the bathroom splashed at little water to wipe the dry tears from her face.

When she exited the terrace door, Mark was sitting out by the pool. He looked disappointed.

"I went to the hotel looking for you and you weren't there. I called your phone and no answer. I was worried." Mark said.

"I'm sorry. I just..."

"I had one of the best nights of my life and you weren't there."

"I'm sorry, Mark, but this is too much for me."

"What is too much?"

"You…this whole thing."

"I don't understand."

"Did you sleep with Ms. Oni?"

"What? Where is that coming from?"

"I feel so stupid." Heather said sitting down at the patio table.

"Why are you saying that? Why are you asking about Ms. Oni?"

"You know why! The rumors about your sex life is always in the limelight."

"What does that have to do with Ms. Oni?"

"Did you sleep with her or not?"

"No. I have not."

"What about other women you have worked with?"

"Is that what this is about! You think I am sleeping with you because we work together?"

"Well, have you slept with other women you've worked with or not?"

"Yes, I have before, but that was a long time ago."

"So, what am I to you? Am I a piece of convenient ass?"

"I can't believe you would say something like that."

"I don't think we knew each other well enough to start this and now that I am..."

"You're what?"

"Nothing...look, let's just finish this tour." Heather stood up as if she was closing the conversation.

"What is that supposed to mean?" Mark looked up at Heather.

"I don't want to do this with you anymore. I know you have plenty of other options. You don't need me."

"Heather, don't be like that." Mark candidly pleaded.

"Let's go. I see you've parked a chopper on my father's helipad."

"Yea," Mark chuckled looking back at it, "that is cool as hell. I didn't know your pops had one. I mean...he said I could land it to pick you up."

"Yea, so let me say goodbye to my parents so we can go."

"OK. I will wait right here for you."

Heather disappeared into her father's massive estate and told her parents goodbye. She managed to escape before any of their friends figured out that Mark B. was in their backyard, not that they cared, but the less who knew, the better. The helicopter was gearing up when Heather came back to the terrace.

"You ready?" Mark asked.

"Yes."

He grabbed her by the hand and led her through the bushy trail out to the helipad that her dad frequently used. When they were inside, Heather put on her head gear and put on her seatbelt. Mark gave the pilot the queue to go and they were off to the airport.

Heather intentionally did not look at Mark. She had a lot to think about. She felt bad though. She had yet to congratulate him on the music awards he received. She broke the ice.

"Congratulations on your successful night." Heather said through the headphone.

"Thank you, Ms. Grand." Mark said and didn't seem interested in the conversation.

Heather took note and didn't say another word. He was upset. Hell, so was she. She had accused him of hoeing around and she felt like those women made her a groupie for falling for his charm. Either way, the vibe in the air was eerie.

When they arrived in Boston, Heather was given

a key to her own room and her bags were taken to the room by the bellman. Inside, it was quiet and lonely. When she went to check out her view, she was interrupted by a knock at the door. Through the peephole, Heather saw Mark.

"Hey." Heather said as she opened the door.

"Is everything OK in your room?" Mark looked over her shoulder.

"Yes. Thank you." Heather answered.

An awkward silence was broken when a woman from down the hall recognized Mark B. She screamed and ran toward him. "Mark!" she yelled.

"Oh, shit." Mark pushed Heather inside the room and closed the door. The girl outside the room knocked on the door, but Mark and Heather ignored it.

"Who was that?" Heather asked.

"A fan, I guess."

"Well, looks like my room has been compromised. She's going to think this is your room all night." Heather chuckled.

"I know. You're going to need to get a different room."

"Dammit, Mark."

"I'm sorry. I came to see you." Mark shrugged his shoulders.

"Why? I told you we can't see each other like that."

"I know what you said, but I am a little persistent about what I want."

"Oh, well, you'll have to slow your roll on me. I don't know if I can handle being with you."

"Why?"

Heather holds her palm out in the direction of the door indicating the fan that just tried to mow him down.

"Oh, that." He smirked.

"Yea, that."

"What do you want me to do? Give up everything?" Mark sounded serious.

"No. The reason I love you is because of who you are."

"You said, love." Mark perked up.

"You know what I mean."

"I will give you some space, Heather. I will respect your boundaries, but I don't have to like it."

"Thank you." Heather kissed Mark one last time on the cheek.

"I am going to show you that I want a relationship with you and that these women out here don't mean anything to me."

"It's not about those women." Heather sort of lied.

Mark continued, "And most importantly, that you are not just a piece of convenient ass. That really hurt my feelings that you think I would do that."

"Mark, I said that because that is how I felt. I don't want to ever feel like I can't say what I feel, no matter how good or bad it may make you feel."

Heather said.

"So, the Friend Zone it is. Let's get through this tour. I want you to work with me on some other projects that I have coming up." Mark said.

"What do you mean?" Heather was intrigued.

"It means that I want you to consider joining my team and being a writer on my next venture."

Heather sat down on the sofa to get comfortable. She wasn't planning on talking to Mark this long, but it sounded like they could actually talk about something other than their relationship.

"What new venture?"

"I have a business partner who wants me to join his film production team."

"Are you asking me to be a writer for a film?"

"Yes."

"What kind of film?"

"It's a drama film. We're going to have a meeting about it in a week or so. I wanted to throw it out there before I went looking for someone else." Mark concluded.

"I appreciate the opportunity."

"Is that a yes?"

"It's a yes. I've always wanted to work on a film."

"Do you have script writing under your belt?"

"I've took a class on it in college, but it's nothing I can't get a refresher on."

"Good. I'll keep you in the loop."

"Thanks, now get me a new room!" Heather said ignoring another knock at the door.

"We'll have to chill here for a while. I have to get my team to help clear the floor so we can move undetected."

"Fine. Do you want something to drink? The mini bar is fully stocked. I could use a drink."

"Sure. Now, tell me what happened today that had you biting my head off."

Heather took all of the mini shots bottles of

bourbon from the refrigerator and grabbed two shot glasses from the cabinet and came over to the sofa.

"Whoa, are you planning to get drunk?"

"We'll see!"

"So, what happened?"

Heather rehashed the horrific night she spent on the red carpet with Flosia. Mark had to laugh at how awful Heather described the incident. He made fun of her feet hurting and even the two gossiping women in the dressing room.

"That's not funny!" Heather gave Mark a little punch on his bicep.

"What? Those women were probably old and crusty!" Mark joked.

"Yes, they were!" Heather joined in the joke.

Mark and Heather spent the next couple of hours talking about everything under the sun while turning up drinks in the process. Mark shared his moment receiving his awards.

"It was really a special night. Since my mother passed when I was younger, I take relationships with women to heart. My aunt in New York is all I have and she couldn't make it. It really hurt me that you weren't there." Mark explained.

"I was an emotional wreck. I am so sorry. If you'll invite me, then I'll be at your next one." Heather said tucking her arm under Mark's arm to snuggle.

Mark received a text and then there was a knock at the door.

"That's Manny, are you good?"

"Yea, I'll be fine. I'll grab my things."

"Don't worry. Manny's got your things. Let's just go to the room."

Mark took Heather to the elevator and exited on another floor. He opened the door to the new room and took her to the bedroom. He helped her out of her clothes and put her in bed. When he finished, he kissed on the forehead.

"I felt that." Heather slurred with her eyes closed.

"I hope so. Good night."

"Night, Mark."

He put her cellphone on the nightstand and left the room. Manny was waiting just outside to walk with Mark back to his suite.

"You really like this one, don't you?" Manny said as they went to the adjoining room next door.

"Yea, man."

"What's so special about her, though? I mean, you have had some pretty hot chicks and this one seems so Plain Jane."

"That's what I love about her. She's the sexiest Plain Jane I know." Mark said when he went inside his room.

"This is a first." Manny said from the threshold.

"There is a first for everything, and I like how this first one feels." Mark said before he closed the door.

For the next several months, Heather and Mark became the best of friends and spent all of their time together. Mark respected Heather's wishes by not attempting to push up on her. They maintained friendly and professional boundaries. The rumors continued, but Heather was not consumed by them because she knew the truth. Her and Mark were really friends and she absolutely enjoyed that.

"Hi, Justice." Heather said.

"Hey, girl! You've been all over the globe. Where are you now?"

"I'm back in LA. I am about to transition to a new project with Mark."

"You are finally about the start that film that you told me about some months ago."

"Yes. I am about to put in my resignation at Musiq."

"Why? You better not put all of your eggs in that man's basket."

"What? I can't do both. They hired me to travel and I don't want to travel with another artist. This job with Mark was enough. They can let someone else do this. Besides, like I said, I can't do both."

"Your column is so freaking hot! Are you sure you want to give that up for a film job."

"Don't make it sound so boring."

"It does sound boring. You should figure out how you can do both because I love reading your work."

"I will think about it. I can't make any promises though."

"Didn't you sign a contract with Musiq?"

"I did, but it was not a termed contract. It was just an agreement of terms and the job offer. I am free to leave whenever I want. Besides, those bitches have bccn jealous of me and Mark since I started."

"Who?"

"The other writers. I don't go into the office much, but when we bump into each other on the road, I always feel like they give me attitude."

"Well, don't let that be the reason and since you put a comfortable distance between you and Mark, don't put all of your trust in that either."

"That's just it. I trust him more now than before."

"Why?"

"I get to see everything. I even get to see him around women, groupies, fans, or whoever. He is consistent with how he deals with people."

"What makes that so trustworthy?" Justice asked.

"Before, I was listening to gossip and making assumptions."

"Oh, so, now that you're on the inside, you can trust sleeping with him again?"

"I didn't say all of that, but if he were to have a

weak moment, I wouldn't hold it against him."

"So, what you're saying is, a sister still has needs!"

"Exactly and it's been a minute!"

"Well, be careful. You two have been on and off, so keep your options open."

Heather laughed that bit of advice and they said their goodbyes. Heather was about to do some shopping and enjoy her afternoon. Her and Mark had not shared hotels since they decided to be in the friend zone, so that gave Heather a little more freedom.

At the mall, Heather went into her favorite boutique and looked at an evening dress to wear to the tour wrap up party. Mark was throwing the party in LA with the entire crew. It was most likely going to turn into an industry party, and Heather wanted to look the part and find comfortable shoes.

"Hi, Ms. Grand." The sales representative

recognized her.

"Do I know you?" Heather asked hesitantly.

"No, but I read your column. You've been on tour with Mark B. James. I love him."

"Oh, okay. That's great. It's been a wonderful tour."

"You're a great writer. I know it must have been hard working for someone like him."

"It was a good experience."

"Are you guys going out?"

Heather rolled her eyes and started to walk away. What started off as an innocent conversation with a sales associate became a gossiping probe. Heather didn't buy anything. She left the store and caught a taxi to Rodeo Drive, the place where seeing a famous person was nothing to bat an eye at.

Inside the cab, Heather called Mark. "What should I wear tonight?"

"Something sexy and short."

"Sexy and short?" Heather chuckled.

"I think you look hot in short dresses. And make it red."

"Why red?"

"That's my favorite color." He said.

"I like red. It's a power color."

"Exactly. You did your damn thing on this tour and I think you deserve to stand out from the crowd."

"Well, I may have a hard time finding something short and red. I wasn't thinking that specific."

"Where are you now?"

"I am headed to Rodeo Drive."

"I'll meet you there. I know the perfect place."

"Okay."

Heather sighed in relief knowing that she would not have to find the dress on her own. If anyone had ideas and connections, it was Mark B. When the cab driver arrived on Rodeo, Heather saw Manny standing in front of Henry Bendel's.

Heather stepped out of the cab and walked over to him.

"Hi, Manny."

"What the hell are you doing in a cab?"

"What?" Heather looked back at the cab as if something was deathly wrong with it.

"You know we have car service for you. Use it." Manny demanded.

"I just thought it would be easier to fit in without it."

"You are one of us now. You don't fit in. Besides, Mark would have my ass if he knew you were in that damn thing." He paid the cab driver a hefty tip to get the hell out of there.

"He doesn't have to know." Heather smirked.

"You're lucky he wasn't out here." Manny looked over at the boutique. "He's in there. Go ahead, he's waiting for you."

Heather went into the boutique and Mark had already set up the dressing room for her to try on the dresses.

"Right this way, Ms. Grand." The sales associate said.

"Thank you." Heather winked at Mark who was sitting on the waiting area sofa watching her.

"Make sure you come out when you try them on."

"Yes, sir, captain, sir." Heather teased.

One dress after another, Heather tried on what the associate brought her. It was the last dress that Mark actually stood up for, "That's the one."

Heather looked at her body in the dress and turned around to see the rear view. She pretended to have on heels and spun around to face Mark, "I like this one, too."

The sales associate was already on top of the shoes. She was relieved that he brought one and a half inch pumps and not the six inch heels. Mark must have warned the associate beforehand.

"I like those." Mark pointed at a pair.

"Why do you like those?" Heather questioned looking at the other pair she thought looked fine with the dress.

"Because, they go perfectly with these." Mark said as he opened a jewelry box that displayed the most beautiful necklace and earrings.

"Oh, my. These are gorgeous." Heather caressed the jewels.

"Are we done here?" Mark asked closing the box.

"I think so." Heather confirmed.

"Good. Put everything on this card." Mark handed the associate a credit card. "Let's have this meeting with the film crew, then get ready for the party tonight."

"Sounds good to me." Heather said.

Heather transformed back into her clothes while Mark waited for the dress and accessories to be wrapped up. Heather was prepared to pay for the items herself, but as usual, Mark beat her to it.

"I was going to buy my own outfit this time." Heather sounded offended.

"You're welcome." Mark said sarcastically.

Heather gave him an elbow on the side as they walked out onto the street to meet Manny.

"Thanks." Heather said before sliding into the rear seat of the SUV.

♠♠♠

When they arrived at the nightclub, the line was wrapped around the corner. Heather took a deep breath as she squeezed Mark's knee as they pulled up to the curb.

"Are you OK?" Mark asked.

"Yea, I just get anxious at clubs. You know they are not my thing."

"I know, but we won't be here long. We have the follow up production meeting first thing."

"Good."

Manny was already at the door ready to open it. Mark tapped on the door to give him the go to let them out. The red carpet was laid out on the ground to pave the way into the club. When the doors opened, Mark stepped out first, then he turned to take Heather's hand to escort her out. The fans clapped when they walked through. Some gave fist bumps, pats on the back, while others gave genuine smiles to both of them.

Inside the club, it was crowded from wall to wall. Manny and the team escorted Mark and Heather to the VIP section in the club. Mark put Heather between him and Manny. He held onto her waistline, and she held onto his hand to ensure he had her safely.

"You are going to make me take the next exit on this friend zone." He said.

"Huh?" Heather turned around to hear him over the music.

"Nevermind." Mark said and patted Heather on

the ass.

"Ooh!" Heather was surprised by the gesture and hopped forward a bit.

In the VIP section, they had plenty of room to move around and enjoy themselves. Heather was surprised to see her best friend already there. "Justice!" Heather turned and looked at Mark who had a smirk on his face. She didn't know who to hug first.

"Hi, sis." Justice gave her best friend a hug.

"Hi!" Heather said.

"I knew you would be shocked to see me. It was a last minute plan to fly out here."

"Uh, yea! I had no idea. Hi, Darrin." Heather gave him a hug, too.

"Hi, Heather." Darrin said and gave Mark a fist bump.

The night couldn't be more perfect for Heather. The celebration was a night she would remember. The champagne bottles were popping all night.

Manny even found some time to dance a two step to a 90s R&B jam.

"Let's dance." Mark said.

Before she could answer, Mark had already pulled her up onto her feet. When they reached the dance floor, Mark put his hands around Heather's waist and pulled her close.

"What did you say earlier?" Heather whispered closely in his ear.

"I said that I am ready to exit the friend zone."

Heather did not reply. Instead she pulled herself into Mark and allowed their energy to mingle. It had been months since she had felt him this close to her. It felt good and their chemistry was boiling over. Heather's heart and mind were in conflict.

"Stop being afraid." Mark said in her ear.

Heather laid her head on his chest and inhaled his cologne. It was one of her favorites. She smiled. The moment was perfect until there were awkward sounds that rang out. "Pow! Pow! Pow!"

Mark pulled Heather to the floor and covered her with his body. It felt like he weighted a ton. When the shots stopped she tried to move, but Mark wasn't moving.

"Mark!"

Heather heard Manny's voice, but she couldn't see anything.

Manny pulled Mark's body off of Heather. "Call 9-1-1!"

Mark was shot and blood was gushing from his side. Manny applied pressure to the wound.

"Stay with us!" Heather told Mark as she kissed his lips, "Stay with me, baby."

The club was in chaos and there were other people hurt in the club. She looked around for Justice. She seen her leaned over a body rocking back and forth.

"Justice!" Heather went to her best friend.

"He's dead!" Justice sobbed.

"What?!" Heather screamed.

The faint sound of sirens could be heard in the background. The club was full of people who stood around looking at the mayhem.

Heather went over to Mark who was starting to fade. The EMT rushed over with a kit and started immediately trying to save Mark.

"He's lost a lot of blood we have to get him out of here." EMT said.

Heather was torn, but she had to go with Mark. Mark was strapped to the stretcher and taken out of the club within minutes. Heather rode in the ambulance and saw Mark fighting for his life. He was fading fast. Heather could not believe what was happening. One minute she was thinking sweet thoughts about him and seconds later, he was moments away from death. A perfect night had turned into a nightmare.

At the hospital, Heather and Manny, both covered in blood, had to wait for Mark to get out of surgery. The waiting room began to fill with the rest of the tour crew. Heather sat in the corner at a distance from everyone. She shook her head thinking about how close she was to being shot in that club. The anger made her cry and she couldn't contain it. Manny came over to comfort her.

"Hey, he's going to pull through. He's a fighter, if I ever knew one."

"He took that bullet trying to save me." Heather sobbed.

"And he wouldn't have had it any other way." Manny said patting Heather on the shoulder.

"My best friend's fiancé died."

"The attorney?" Manny asked.

"Yes. I feel so bad for her."

"I'm so sorry." Manny said.

"Who would do something like this? Did they target us?" Heather said.

"I don't know, sweetie. We have a lot to find out. I have my ears in the street now. Fuck what the cops are doing. We are going to find out who did this."

"Don't do anything crazy, Manny."

"We are going to get to the bottom of this. That's a promise. That bullet could have been for any one of us." Manny said matter of fact.

Heather looked up and saw the doctor approach. Everyone stood up, but the doctor came over to Heather.

"He's out of surgery, but still in critical condition. The bullet entered his back, hit the spinal cord and was lodged in his lung. We do not know the extent of the damage until he is stable."

"Can I see him?" Heather asked.

"Yes, but only two at a time." The doctor said looking at the crowd of people standing around him.

"Thank you, doctor." Heather said.

"Heather, you go in. I have some shit to do." Manny said as he looked down at his phone.

"Manny, be careful."

"I will. Go in there and be there when he wakes up." Manny said.

"Okay."

Heather was headed to Mark's room when she saw Justice come through the hospital door. Heather ran over to her and hugged her best friend.

"I'm so sorry."

"I don't know what to do, Heather." Justice said and sobbed in her friend's arms.

Heather did not know what to say. She could only hug and comfort her friend. It was unfair. This was not how she imagined the night ending. The night was so optimistic. This tragedy would scar her for life, she thought. It further supported her dislike for the celebrity lifestyle. It was a magnet for trouble and tragedy.

"Where is Mark?" Justice asked.

"He's in ICU." Heather said.

"How bad was it?"

"Bad."

"How bad?"

"The bullet hit his spine."

"How bad is the damage?"

"It's too soon to tell."

"Have you been in to see him?"

"I was about to go when I saw you."

"Go. Go see about your man, girl." Justice tried to smile with the sniffles.

Heather hugged her best friend and went to Mark's room. When she arrived, a police officer was posted up at the door. The eerie sound of the machines beeped. A tube was taped to his mouth and the oxygen machine pushed air into Mark's lungs. He looked worse than she expected. Heather couldn't hold back her tears. She sat in the chair next to his bed and grabbed his hand.

"You have to pull through this. We have too much shit to do." Heather said squeezing his hand.

She laid her head on the side of the bed and said a prayer. It wasn't something that she did often, but it was no time like to present to call in a favor. Mark did not deserve this and he damn sure had more work to do.

Hours later, Manny arrived. "Any change?"

"No." Heather whispered.

"I found out some information."

"What did you find?"

"It was a hit on your girl's fiancé."

"What? Darrin? Why?"

"Now, I don't know all of that and to be honest, I don't want to know."

"Then how did Mark get shot?"

"That motha' fucka was a bad shooter." Manny said.

"A bad shooter! What the hell is that supposed to mean? Someone made a mistake!"

"Basically. That hit on your girl's fiancé was no doubt related to some street shit. I don't know what he did or who he fucked over, but apparently, it got his ass killed." Manny said.

"This is not happening to me. I don't live this life?"

"This life?" Manny was agitated.

"Yes, this guns and clubs shit. I don't live looking over my shoulder."

"What are you saying? You are too good for my boy?" Manny was getting angry.

"I am saying, I don't live looking over my shoulder and that is what I meant."

"Your girl need to watch her own back because whatever her man was into, she may still be a target."

"What?" Now, Heather was getting agitated.

"Look, if you are going to bail on my boy, then go ahead and leave now. I can handle this." Manny pulled out his cellphone and starting sliding the screen.

"Wait a damn minute. I almost got shot. Do you understand that? And I love Mark, I am not going anywhere. Check your attitude."

"That's all I need to know. Either you're in or your out. I don't need no soft ass woman around him. He needs your support so fuckin' give it to him and stop bitchin'!"

Heather was appalled, but she kept quiet. Manny was right. Mark needed her to be strong and focus on him. He did take a bullet for her. She owed him her loyalty, especially now.

Heather pulled out her cellphone and sent a text to Justice.

She texted: "We need to talk."

CHAPTER SIX

"What do you mean he was a target?" Justice said.

"It sounds like Darrin was involved with something and they came in there to shoot him." Heather explained.

"This sounds like bullshit." Justice said.

"I am just telling what the word on the street is. I don't know much else."

"What am I supposed to do with this information, Heather?"

"You're a reporter, you know what to do."

"I can't go to the police with these speculations."

"I don't want Manny's name in it. I don't know who he had to shake up for that information. I just wanted you to know it wasn't random. You have to watch your back, sis." Heather concluded.

"Watch my back? I don't even know from whom."

"When you get home, dig into his shit and find out. Just be careful."

"I will. I am flying out tomorrow. It's going to be a few days before they release his body."

"Where are they sending him?"

"They are sending him to his parents in DC."

"I am so sorry this happened."

"Me, too. I don't even know what to think. I have to make some calls and see if I can get to the bottom of this."

"Like I said, be careful. Keep me updated."

"I will, sis. I love you so much. I don't say that hardly enough."

"I know. I love you, too." Heather looked at her phone and saw a call from her mother coming in, "Mom is calling."

"My mom must have told her. Sorry, she's probably going to fuss since you haven't called her."

"Thanks for that heads up. Talk to you later." Heather said.

"Okay." Justice said.

Heather answered the incoming call, "Hi, mom."

"I wish you would call me when things like this happen. Are you alright?" Her mom asked.

"Yes, mom. I am fine."

"Mark. Is he alright?" Her mom asked.

"He's still unconscious, but he is out of surgery."

"What happened, dear?"

"Someone came in and shot into the area we were in."

"Were they targeting someone?"

"I don't know all of the details yet." Heather lied.

"When are you coming home?"

"Mom, I don't live in Atlanta. My home is New York, and I am not going anywhere until Mark is okay."

"I see. Can I do anything to help?"

"No, I am going to be fine. Just tell dad and my baby sis that I'm fine. I'll keep you updated."

"Okay. I love you." Her mom said.

"Love you too, mom." Heather said.

The last thing Heather needed was her mother going back and gossiping to her friends about what happened. It's best that it was kept quiet. When Heather made it back to the room, Manny was asleep on the chair that was next to the bed. Heather went near the window and looked out at the highway's view from this hospital. Cars swiftly drove east and west as people were going about their lives. Heather realized that she was one of those people only hours ago. She was happy and satisfied with where she was and who she was spending her time with. Now, she was standing in a hospital room with hope in her heart that she can get that back.

The sofa near the window became her bed for the night. When daylight broke, the sun shined through the curtains and woke her up. The nurse came in to check on Mark's vitals which had not changed.

"Good morning." Heather said to the nurse.

"Hi." The nurse was short.

"I said, good morning." Heather reiterated.

"I'm sorry. Good morning." The nurse said, then left the room.

"Bitch. No bedside manners." Heather said before getting up to go over to the bed to check on Mark. She grabbed his hand, leaned in to kiss him on the forehead, "Good morning, my love."

Heather felt a slight squeeze from Mark when she rubbed his head after her kiss.

"Hmmm," Mark tried to speak but the tube was on his mouth.

Heather removed it.

"Be nice." Mark said groggily and smiled.

"I was." Heather said with a smile. She grabbed her phone and sent a text to Manny. He must have left the room in the middle of the night. She pushed the nurse button.

"Yes." The same nurse came in.

"Please get the doctor. Mark is awake."

"Yes, ma'am." The nurse said and rushed out of the room.

Manny came back in before the doctor. "He's awake?"

"He's conscious, but he's still weak." Heather said.

"That's my dude! I knew he would fight." Manny said.

The doctor came in and did an assessment. Just as Heather and Manny began to celebrate, they found out that Mark had paralysis.

"What do you mean? I can't walk?" Mark struggled to talk.

"It may be temporary. We don't know." The doctor said.

"May be temporary sounds like it could be permanent, too."

"That is a possibility. Let's give it a couple days to see if there is any change. You have to give your body a chance to heal itself. I just wanted to give you the facts as they stand."

"That's some bullshit!" Mark suddenly got angry and pushed the table away from his bed. It crashed up against the wall. "Everybody get out! Get out!"

Heather put her head down and followed everyone out of the room. When the door closed, they heard Mark yell obscenities, then they heard him sobbing loudly. Manny walked away. He couldn't stay and listen to his boss go through those emotions. Heather's heart was hurt all over again.

She felt so guilty for not being the one shot. That should have been her in there. She leaned up against the wall and slid down to the floor in tears. Mark didn't want to see her. He probably regretted saving her life. Heather gathered herself and stormed out of the hospital.

"Where are you going?" Manny yelled after Heather from the waiting room.

She ignored him and kept going. It was nothing she could do for him like this. Besides, he didn't want to see her. He didn't want to see anyone. The disgust in his voice, she'll never forget that.

Heather took a cab back to the hotel. She had to get out of the bloody clothes, take a shower, and clear her head. The ride to the hotel was surreal because the same highway she watched people ride along the night before, she was now on it. Assumingly living life, but in actuality, her life was in disarray. Nothing was as it should be.

Back at the hotel, Heather called Musiq and

updated Ms. Innis and Dan about what was going on. She ultimately told them that she was resigning. She did not want the job anymore.

"Why? Your column is the hottest thing on the shelf right now."

"I know. This isn't about my writing, Ms. Innis." Heather said.

"Then what is it about? You can take a leave if you just need time."

"No, I've made up my mind. I am going to do some other writing outside of the hip hop genre for a while." Heather said.

"Thankfully, we're in between tours and you were not expected to release another article for weeks. I have to find a replacement. So, it's true."

"What's that?"

"You're going to work for Mark B. James."

"At this point, I don't know what I am going to do. Mark is in the fight of his life. The last thing I am thinking about is working for him."

"Aight, then. I guess, I wish you the best."

"That's all I ask. I know where to reach you if I need anything."

"Sure thing. By the way, you and Mark make handsome couple."

"Ms. Innis, it's not…"

"Look, you don't work for Musiq anymore. You don't have to hide anything. If you love the man, then go for it."

"Thanks. I wasn't expecting that from you."

"Why? You think I am a gossiping transsexual that wants your man?"

"No. I just thought that you didn't really like me from the beginning."

"I had my reservations, but you did your damn thing with that column so I have to give you props."

"Well, I appreciate that, Ms. Innis. I will keep you updated."

"Thanks and give Mark my best. If you ever

want to come back to Musiq, then you know I got you."

Heather was shocked by how well that went. It was definitely a load off her back. Then she thought about the fact that Mark may not be able to do anything for a while or possibly forever. That meant she'd be working on this film without him. She didn't want to even think about that. For now, all she wanted to think about was him getting better.

Pretending like she had some life to live, Heather decided to go out to the beach and think. She didn't know where else to go. Manny had been calling her phone consistently, but she just ignored him. If something changed, she figured he'd leave a message. To ease his anxiety, she sent a text and told him where she was. Hoping he'd leave her be.

The afternoon sun glistened over the Pacific Ocean like sparking water. Heather went to the shore and walked into the ocean only thinking about the endless view ahead. There was something about the ocean that always fascinated her. Beyond what she could see, there was something. The life underwater was meaningful enough, but across these waters, was life. Continents of people. Heather became inspired and grateful for her life. The tour with Mark had opened up her eyes to different cultures all over the world. Some of the places they went, it was her first time and she enjoyed those moments with him. She wanted that life. The traveling, the dining, and creating memories. She wasn't willing to give that up so easily. And she wasn't going to let this situation put a wedge between them. Heather watched different people at the beach enjoying themselves, playing with their kids...she wanted that. Eventually, she gathered her things and went back to the hospital.

When she arrived, Manny was asleep in the waiting room, in the same bloody clothes. Heather went to him, "Manny."

"Hey, Heather. What's up? You alright?" Manny said in a sleepy voice.

"Yea, and you need to leave and shower. I'll be here." Heather said.

"You sure?" Manny said sitting up and leaning forward in the chair.

"Yea, it looks like the rest of the crew has left you, so I'll stick around."

"It can be like that. This celebrity life is fickle. People only stick around for the glitz and glam."

"I see. Has he asked to see anyone yet?" Heather was hopefully.

"No." Manny said.

"No problem. You go ahead to the hotel and get some rest. I'll call you if anything changes." Heather said.

"Thanks. Call me if anything, I mean anything changes." Manny demanded.

"I will."

"And make sure to keep those reporters out of here. Don't talk to anyone, not even the staff here. They are all vultures."

"I know. I'm a journalist, so I know how this works."

"Oh, I forget. Nothing against you."

"I got it. Now, get out of here. You smell like two days ago." Heather waved her hand back and forth in front of her nose.

"Oh, shut up." Manny said and gave Heather a big bear hug.

"Ewwww! Get off of me!" She laughed.

"Aight, I'm out. I'll be back soon."

"Don't rush."

Manny left and Heather sat in the waiting area with her laptop. She opened it and started writing. Before she knew it, she had started writing about the day and a life of a hip hop artist. She opened one of her personal blogs pages and posted it:

"If you do not know what it's like to be a celebrity in this world, then I am about to tell you how it is. It's not all fun! I went from being behind the scenes and behind all of my words to being in front of the camera over night. It was a dramatic shock and I was only a journalist. Working as a journalist is supposed to be a faceless job. People don't have to know your face to like reading your work. Being a celebrity is different. People have to see you, touch you, and be all up in your face. For what? To give them something to bop their head to, to give them a song to sing, or to give them something to dance to? No one realizes how dangerous this job is. I just witnessed my friend, Mark B. James get shot, gunned down in a club. That was not in the job description."

Heather hit the post button, then shared the blog on her social media page and within minutes her phone was buzzing with notifications. She couldn't decipher if they were Mark's fans or hers, but they all wanted to put in their two cents. One reader responded:

"He gets paid a lot of money as a celebrity. If he doesn't want to be a target, then he should find another career."

Another responded:

"Grand, you're a good one! I couldn't do that job and be so close to all of the drama. It's not all that it's cracked up to be. You're lucky you didn't get shot!"

Another responded:

"Stop complaining. You're getting paid. I wish I could follow Mark B. James around and get paid. Your job is the shit!"

Heather couldn't believe the mixed opinions about her post, but people just didn't get it. All they saw was the fame and money. The lifestyle looked glamourous and it has been, as far as Heather was concerned, but that did not make it safe. Heather decided not to reply to any of the comments. It was just interesting to see how many people actually read it.

After reading over many comments, Heather started to get hungry. The hospital cafeteria was down the hall. It was the only option. One the way, she decided to peek into Mark's room. When she walked passed the window, she saw the ill-mannered nurse sitting next to the bed talking to Mark. Heather turned abruptly with jealously and anger in her heart. She wanted to leave the hospital, but she couldn't. She promised Manny she'd stay. Before she made it back out to the waiting room, the nurse came out of the room.

"Ms. Grand." The nurse called out.

Heather turned and looked at the nurse.

"He is asking for you." The nurse said.

The anxiety should have dissipated, but Heather was nervous about seeing Mark. Was he going to end their friendship? Was he going to cut her out of his life? She didn't know, but she was about to find out.

She tapped on the door before going in, "Hey you. It's me." Heather whispered.

"Come in." Mark said.

Heather walked over to the side of the bed and waited for Mark to speak. He hesitated for a while, as if he was trying not to show any emotion.

"I'm sorry…" He began.

"It's o…" Heather interrupted.

"No, it's not okay. I should have never yelled at you or Manny like that. I know you two are the only one's out there supporting me right now. I have to get through this and I need you."

"I'm not going anywhere."

"What happened, Heather? What happened at the club?"

"Manny said they were targeting Darrin."

"The attorney?"

"Why?"

"I don't know. Manny didn't get details."

"Where's he at?" Mark questioned.

"I sent him to the hotel to shower. He wouldn't leave. Do you want me to call him?" Heather asked.

"No. I want to spend some time with you. We have some planning to do."

"Planning?" Heather asked.

"Yes, please sit down."

Heather sat down in the same chair she saw the nurse sitting in.

"I need you to find us a place out here. I ain't buying that doctor's prognosis bullshit. I'm walking out of this hospital! The nurse tickled my feet and I felt a faint tingle, but not enough to try and walk."

"That's great, but wait. A place? You want to live together?"

"Well, I mean, unless you want to find your own

place, that's fine with me, but for this film project, I don't want to be flying back and forth out here. So, you can…wait a minute! No, you can't. You're staying out here with me." Mark cracked a smile.

"The film project is still on?" Heather asked.

"Hell, yeah! This little setback is not going to put me out of business. I have to keep moving if I am going to get over this." Mark said.

Heather smiled while in thought about her living in LA with Mark. It just did not seem real. What were they now? An item? "So, are we an item?"

"No. I am not an item to you!" Mark tried to laugh, but he grabbed his lung in pain.

"Ooh, are you okay?"

"Yea, can you hand me that extra pillow?" Mark pointed at the foot of the bed.

"Here ya go." Heather gave Mark the pillow and he tucked it between his side and the bed.

"Whenever I cough or laugh, I will have to hold this pillow to help keep my lungs from expanding.

It hurts like hell."

"I'm so sorry." Heather said and she couldn't prevent the tears from forming.

"Hey, don't do that. I wouldn't have had it any other way. If I had lost you, I'd never be able to live with myself." Mark said grabbing Heather's hand.

"How do you think I feel?" Heather said whipping her tears.

"I know, but that is what a man is supposed to do for someone he cares about. It was my job to protect you and I did. I chose your life that night and I would choose it again." Mark said.

"But now look at you." Heather said.

"This is nothing. I had to get over my feelings and accept what's about to happen. I have to work hard to get back on my feet. Simple as that."

"Manny said you are a fighter." Heather said.

"I came into this world fighting. I've had a lot of loss growing up in the streets of New York, this is just another jab, but I'll recover. I'm sorry if I scared you." Mark said.

Manny came through the door at that moment.

"Hey, I was about to put an APB out on Heather. She left the post." Manny joked.

"Nah, we're just talking." Mark said.

Manny came over and gave Mark dap.

"We're good?" Mark looked at Heather.

"Yes, Mr. James, we're good." Heather smiled.

"Good. Let me chop it up with Manny for a minute. I need some information about what happened. The less you know the better." Mark winked.

"I understand. I was about to go grab something to eat. You want anything?" Heather looked at Manny and Mark. They both shook their heads, no. Heather left and thought about finding something on the outside instead. She was feeling a little better now that she and Mark hashed out their emotions about the shooting, but moving together, that just opened her up to a plethora of other feelings.

On the ride to a nearby restaurant, she thought about the idea of living with Mark. Was that the move she wanted to make? Why did it seem like she was doubting this opportunity to be with her dream guy? Maybe it was their friendship that she wanted to protect. Or maybe it was the friendship that made it so right? Did she owe him, now? An emotional rollercoaster was forming. She did not know what to do. In times like this she usually called Justice, but with her situation so fresh, it probably wouldn't be a good time to talk about her man problems. So, Heather called her real sister.

"Hi, Tiffany."

"Hey, sis. What's up? I heard some shit went down in LA. You OK?" Tiffany asked.

"Yea, things are good. How's college?"

"You did not call me to talk about college. What's up?" Tiffany was blunt just like her big sister expected her to be.

Tiffany was Heather's only real sister. They were nine years apart and did not have a close relationship because of that. Justice was always more like a sister than Tiffany. Tiffany was the spoiled daddy's girl that Heather used to have to babysit all the time. After Heather moved to New York, they only spoke when they needed to on holidays and at family functions. Heather calling out of the blue was a sign that something was up.

"Okay. I need to ask your advice."

"My advice? This ought to be good." Tiffany hissed.

"Hear me out, okay."

"I'm listening."

Heather ran down the scenario that Mark proposed; which included a synopsis of their relationship over the past months on the tour.

"So, what is the problem?" Tiffany asked.

"The problem is he's laying up in a hospital shot.

Is it a good idea for me to move in with him?"

"Sis, you've been a Mark B. James fan for as long as I can remember. What the hell is the problem? Are you scared he's going to get tired of you and leave you for some other chic?" Tiffany asked seriously.

"I don't know what I am afraid of." Heather lied.

"You don't know. That's bullshit. You know." Tiffany said.

"Okay, maybe I am. Maybe I am not the glamour girl that most celebrities have."

"Heather, you are not that type and if he wanted that type, he'd have it. I'm just saying. You're being paranoid over nothing. Just be yourself. As cliché as that sounds."

"Thanks sis. I know we don't talk much, but I just needed someone to bounce this off of."

Tiffany chuckled, "I know you couldn't talk to Justice. I heard the news about her boyfriend or fiancé, or whatever he was. That's messed up. Did they catch the guy who did it?"

"No. I don't think so." Heather was grateful for her little sister's advice more than she knew.

"Well, I have to get back to this term paper. My freshman year is kicking my ass!" Tiffany said.

"Oh okay, then get to it. I'll talk to you soon. Maybe you can come out during spring break." Heather offered.

"I'll do that. I still have yet to meet Mark B. and my friends will be so jealous." Tiffany said.

Heather had the cab stop at a restaurant that she wanted to dine at. When she sat down at the table she realized that she had received over ten thousand likes and over three thousand comments to her post. Some readers responded:

"Celebrities don't have any privacy and they are vulnerable to the crazies in the world who are jealous of their fame."

"Grand, you're a fool for putting yourself in that position. Count your lucky stars that it's not you laying up in that hospital bed, shot!"

"Tell Mark B that I'm praying for him. #MarkBJames"

"Get a life. Celebrities choose this line of work and that means they have to deal with the pressures and sometimes that can be facing death at the hands of idiots in this world."

"Are you and Mark B dating now? The gossip is you two are getting married. Is that true?"

Heather got a good chuckle out of the last comment she read. This was not the response she expected from her readers. It was interesting to read the different opinions and the genuine concern that some fans had for Mark's condition. Others were out right rude and mean, but that came with the territory.

At the table, she looked over the menu before the server came over. Everything looked delicious and lately, she had not been looking at the price of anything, especially food.

"Hi, ma'am. How are you today?" the server asked.

"I am ok. I appreciate you for asking."

"Can I bring you some wine?"

"No. I'll have some sparking water."

"I'll bring that right out."

When the server left the table, Heather noticed that there was a man sitting at an adjacent table watching her. His phone was in a picture taking position. Heather tried to cover her face with her menu, but she saw a flash anyway. That set her off. She slammed the menu down on the table and went over to the man.

"What are you doing?!" Heather yelled at the man.

"What?" He looked dumbfounded.

"Why are you taking my picture?" Heather tried to snatch the phone.

"I am not taking your picture." He insisted and protected his phone.

"Yes, you were. I saw you."

"No, you didn't." He said.

"Let me see!" Heather demanded.

"I don't have to show you anything."

The commotion got the attention of a man in suit, "Is there a problem?" The man asked.

"Yes, this man is invading my privacy by taking pictures of me." Heather explained.

"No, I am not." The man tried to defend himself.

"Sir, we do not allow that kind of thing in our establishment. We have a lot of celebrities in here and we have a 'no photo policy'." The manager said, pointing at the small sign by the entrance. "I'm going to have to ask you to leave."

"Fine." The man pushed back his chair and exited the restaurant.

"Is everything okay, ma'am? Can I get you anything?" the man said.

"No. I think I'll be okay. I think I should order my meal to go."

"Sure. I'll send your server over."

Heather ordered her meal to go and headed back to the hospital. She tried not to keep looking over her shoulder, but it was pointless. She was officially paranoid.

♠♠♠

Manny was not at the hospital by the time Heather returned. It was actually fairly quiet for such a busy hospital. When she sat down her bag of food on the table near the window, she must have made too much noise because it woke Mark.

"You're back. I was getting worried."

"Worried? Why?"

"I didn't know where you were. I told Manny he has to get someone to be out with you. I don't like you out there alone with all of this drama going on. We still don't know who was behind the shooting."

Heather thought about the man in the restaurant. Why was he trying to take her picture? She couldn't think of a reason why. She was not the celebrity, Mark was.

"Why would someone want to shoot Darrin? He was just an attorney." Heather asked.

"He wasn't just an attorney, babe." Mark said.

"What do you mean, he wasn't just an attorney?"

"He had some street connections." Mark confirmed.

"What kind of street connections?"

"Let's just say, he wasn't on the up and up."

"Oh, my god. My best friend was standing right there next to him. She could have been shot, too."

Heather realized.

"I know and I think the shooter was just shooting rounds to make it look random." Mark said.

"It did look random and as far as the police goes, it doesn't sound like they have a clue." Heather said disappointed.

"The streets are quiet. No one is talking."

"But why would you get shot?"

"That's the million-dollar question. I was no where near that mother fucker!"

"What do we do now?" Heather questioned.

"Nothing. I put a narc out on the streets to see what I can find out. If I get the same story, then we'll have to go with the fact that Darrin was a liability to someone in the streets. To be honest, I don't give a fuck about him like that to be trying to get him justice. I have my own shit to worry about."

"Well, dang. I mean, that was my best friend's

fiancé."

"From the looks of it, you better be glad she wasn't a target, too. So, just let it go, babe." Mark pleaded.

"Okay. I won't bring it up again." Heather promised.

"Let's talk about this blog you got going on." Mark said.

"How did you hear about that?" Heather perked up.

"Words travel fast on social media. Besides, people started downloading my music from iMusical minutes after you posted it." Mark was elated.

"What? Really?"

"Hell, yea, so keep it up. Your blog is bringing some much needed attention to my record sales since the tour ended."

"I didn't expect that. I was just expressing myself."

"That's what you do baby. Just be careful. People start getting in their feelings real quick about your opinions."

"Yea, I know." Heather thought about the man at the restaurant again. She didn't want to tell Mark and worry him about it or feed into her paranoia.

"Doctor says I can check out of here as soon as I can use that damn walker. We need to get a condo set up. Can you manage that? I want to get out of here."

Heather looked over at the aluminum walker sitting next to the bed. She knew it was going to be hard for Mark to use that, but he had to if he wanted to get out of there.

"So, I guess we got work to do, babe." Heather said ambitiously.

"That's right. Now, open your laptop!"

CHAPTER SEVEN

It took about a month for Mark to get the approval from the doctor to leave. In the meantime, Heather found a nice beach house that had a view to die for. Manny had his own suite on the lower level, which was perfect for their makeshift family. When Mark came home from the hospital, the nurse was already there. She was too young and pretty for Heather's taste, but she was supposedly the best.

"Can I get you anything?" Heather asked Mark as she tucked him in.

"Nah, babe. I just want to get comfortable. Put my walker over there. I don't want that shit so close."

"Absolutely, not. You need it by the bed so you can get around." Heather insisted.

"I don't like it." Mark fussed.

"Get over it." Heather said and pushed the walker up to the bed so Mark could grab it if he needed to.

"I'm going to run out and get some things from the store." Heather said.

"Take Manny with you." Mark demanded.

"I don't need Manny. I'll be fine."

"I'd feel better if you did." Mark pleaded.

"Fine. I'll tag the big teddy bear along."

"He better not hear you call him that." Mark smiled.

"Hey. Was that a smile?" Heather asked.

Mark didn't respond. He must have realized what Heather meant.

"I'm trying, babe. I'm really trying."

"I know." Heather kissed Mark on the lips and smiled at the nurse on her way out.

♠♠♠

At the grocery store, Heather and Manny walked through the aisles. When she turned the corner leaving Manny behind, she noticed the fake paparazzi from the restaurant, from a month ago, on the same aisle. Heather looked back to see Manny talking to the butcher, then she walked over to the man.

"Who are you?"

"Excuse me? Who are you?" The man said.

"You know who I am."

"Uh, no I don't." He insisted

"I'm the…" Heather stopped and realized that she was getting loud, "Look, I don't know who you are and why you're following me around, but whatever story you're trying get, you're going about it the wrong way."

"I'm not a reporter."

"Then who are you?"

"A nobody. You are paranoid, lady."

"Ughh!" Heather walked away.

Manny was walking fast toward her, "What's wrong? Who's that guy?" Manny looked passed Heather at the man.

"He's nobody. I thought I knew him from some where."

"Then why are you so mad?" Manny was still focused on the man.

"It's nothing. Let's go. Did you get some meat?" Heather put her arm in Manny's and pulled him along.

Manny turned back one more time and this time he looked the man in his eye.

"I don't like that guy." Manny said.

"What?" Heather laughed.

"It's something in his eyes that ain't right." Manny said.

"Let's go. You're sounding paranoid." Heather tugged at Manny to keep walking.

"Trust me. I know something ain't right with that man. He may not be someone you know, but something is dark inside him."

When they made it to the check out, they both saw the man walking out of the store without making a purchase. Before he went through the door, he turned and looked at Heather, then walked out. Heather and Manny turned to look at each other.

"What the fuck was that about?" Manny said. He left Heather in line with the groceries and went out the door after the man.

"Manny…" Heather tried to call him back, but it was too late. He was gone. Manny turned the corner and was out of sight.

"Is everything alright?" The cashier asked

looking toward the store exit.

"Yea, I think so." Heather said casually.

"You look familiar." The cashier said as she scanned the items.

"Oh, yeah." Heather tried to downplay how the young hip hopping cashier may have seen her on iGram with Mark B.

"That's it! You're Mark B.'s girl."

"Uh, I am not Mark B.'s girl. We work together, yes."

"I knew I recognized you. Can I have your autograph?"

"Well, I…" Heather started.

"Yo, Heather…let's get out of here. We have to get back to the crib."

Heather paid for the groceries in cash and signed the receipt for the cashier. Manny came over to grab the groceries and they left the store in a hurry.

"What's wrong, Manny." Heather said trying to catch up to his fast pace.

"I'll tell you when we get in the truck."

Heather didn't like being scared. She started looking around to make sure nothing or no one was around. Manny put the groceries in the SUV and opened the door for Heather.

"Why are we rushing?" Heather insisted.

"That man is some type of evil."

"Why do you keep saying that?"

"I chased him down and he turned around and dropped some black dust on the ground. That shit had me stopping in my tracks."

"What?"

"Yea, I don't mess around with that shit. I don't know who that guy is, but I don't ever want to see him again."

"It's the second time I seen him since we've been out here in LA."

"What? I thought you didn't know him."

"I don't. He was at a restaurant I was at a while ago. I could have sworn he took my picture."

"Your picture? How did he do that?"

"His smartphone. I thought he was a reporter."

"That man ain't no reporter."

"I guess he's not. Maybe it was a coincidence that he was at the store."

"It didn't seem like that to me."

Heather looked at Manny from the corner of her eye and he was spooked, scared even. It was an awkward ride back to the beach house.

When they arrived, Manny went straight to his room and closed the door. Heather brought the groceries into the kitchen and started preparing dinner.

"Ms. Grand, Mr. James would like to see you." The nurse said as she popped her head into the kitchen.

Heather stopped what she was doing to go see what Mark wanted. On the way to the master bedroom, Heather noticed the nurse adjusting her attire as she walked down the hall to the spare room.

"Yes." Heather said when she went into the room.

"What happened at the store?" Mark asked.

"How did you find out about that?" Heather looked surprised.

"Manny sent me a text. Now, what happened?" He demanded an answer.

"Some guy was giving us an evil look. Manny chased him down the street and he did some voodoo act. Manny was spooked and here we are."

"Why are you acting like this is nothing. Manny does not scare easily. Something is up with that guy and I don't want you out alone anymore."

"I don't need a babysitter, Mark. I can take care of myself."

"You're being stubborn. I just want to protect you, but I can't. Look at me!" Mark sounded defeated.

"I'm sorry, babe. I didn't mean to upset you.

Okay. I will allow security to escort me."

"Thank you. Now come over here and scratch my back. These scars are starting to itch."

"With pleasure."

Heather plopped down on the bed and snuggled up to Mark and scratched his back. "Is that the spot?"

"No, a little to the right."

"Is that it?"

"Nope, a little to the left."

"How about now?"

"Ahhhh, yeah. That's the spot baby. Scratch that spot again." They both laughed at his simple satisfaction.

After dinner, Mark and Heather snuggled and talked for a while before they finally fell asleep. Since the shooting, Heather and Mark had started to develop a different type of relationship. They were more than just friends. They were falling in love.

Over the next month, Heather and Mark collaborated from the condo on the film project. Heather barely left the house because she didn't like the escort. Manny became a super vigilant security guard who looked over his shoulder an extra two or three times. Everything seemed to be going smoothly, until Mark received a call from his entertainment attorney. Heather put her laptop aside as Mark answered the call on speakerphone.

"Hey, Daniel." Mark said.

"Yea, Mark. I have some information that you may not know about." Daniel said.

"What is it?"

"You know they have a suspect for the shooting."

"A suspect. How do you know about that? Have you been part of the investigation?"

"No. I just have my ear to the streets and they plan to make an arrest."

"Who is it?"

"It's Brandon Gilmore."

"Brandon?"

"Yea."

Mark sat up in the bed and could not speak.

"Are you there?" Daniel asked.

"Yeah, man. I'm here."

"Look, don't say or do anything until they actually make the arrest, but I am pretty sure it's a solid case."

"Why would he be after Darrin, though? He doesn't even know him like that."

"I don't know. It's not all clear at this point. I don't even know what evidence they have. I called you as soon as I knew something."

"Thanks, D. I appreciate that. Keep me posted."

"I most definitely will. And how is the recovery going?"

"I am about fifty percent. I can walk with a walker, but I am a long way from being back on stage, my brother."

"Man, this is a tragedy all around. How is the script coming along?"

"Heather and I are working on it as we speak. We'll be ready to present it to the producers in another month or so. I hope to be moving around by then."

"Take your time, Mark. You know life has a way of slowing you down. That tour took a lot out of you. You needed this little break."

"Whatever you say. I am a working man and sitting still just ain't my thing, but I feel you."

"Good. I'll be in touch."

"Yea, thanks for calling."

Heather sat there waiting for more information. She didn't know who Brandon was or why this person was of interest in the case.

"You have to promise not to mention this to Manny." Mark said.

"Promise what?" Heather was confused.

"Brandon is Manny's identical twin brother. He and Manny do the same type of work, but Brandon has been bouncing around a lot."

"Why?"

"He has a bit of a temper. He used to work with me first, but he couldn't keep his attitude under control, so I fired him. When I fired him, he was black balled. No one else on my level wanted to really work with him."

"But why would he shoot Darrin?" Heather inquired.

"I don't know, baby. That is what I need to find out."

"How do you plan to keep this from Manny?"

"I am not supposed to know so he can't find out from me. I have to do what my attorney said in this case. I don't want to get dragged into court. I don't got time for that bullshit."

"But that's his brother."

"I know. Brandon is in some deep shit and I

don't want Manny being pulled into it trying to save his sorry ass."

Heather couldn't argue with that. Manny was one of the good guys. She did not want him dragged into a murder case. "I understand."

"Now, let me show you what I've been practicing every time you step out on your errands."

"What?"

Mark stands up from the bed and takes two steps forward and two steps back without the walker. Heather started to beam with excitement at Mark's progress.

"Oh my god! Yes!" Heather did everything thing, but jump on his back. She jumped up and down and screamed with joy.

Manny came running along with the nurse to see what all of the commotion was about. By the time they got there, Heather was on the bed in Mark's lap kissing his lips passionately.

"What's wrong?" Manny asked barging into the room.

"My baby is taking steps without his walker."

"That's what's up!" Manny came over and gave Mark a fist bump.

The nurse smiled from the doorway and didn't say anything. She nodded and left the room.

"What's up with her?"

"Nah, I told her that this is her last week. I don't need her anymore."

"Are you sure baby?"

"Yes. I think *you* can handle me from now on."

"Handle you?" Heather smiled.

"Yes, handle me." Mark put Heather's hand on erected penis.

Heather's eyes lit up with embarrassment because Manny was still in the room.

"Ahh, man, that's too much information for me." Manny laughed and turned to leave the room. On his way out, he lifted his fist in the air and said,

"My boy is back!"

Mark and Heather smiled at each other and kissed to seal the moment. Heather was elated. Her joy was overwhelming and Mark saw the emotion on her face.

"What's wrong?"

"I have just replayed the past few months of my life through my head and I cannot believe that I'm here where I've wanted to be. To think I almost lost you is still heart wrenching."

"Let's not think about the past. The future is what we have to look forward to."

"Yes. And we are about to blow their minds with this project." Heather confirmed.

"Project? I am not talking about work. I am talking about us."

Mark managed to wiggle Heather off his lap and he slid down on the floor on one knee. It happened so fast that Heather could not even think to breath.

From his robe, Mark revealed a stunning

diamond and said, "Ms. Heather Grand, I love you and I want to spend the rest of my life with you. Will you be my wife?"

Tears were falling uncontrollably from Heather's face, as she managed to say, "Yes."

Mark slid the large diamond ring on Heather's left ring finger. She stared at it for what seemed like an eternity.

"Is the ring, OK?" Mark finally asked.

"Of course, it is beautiful." She grabbed Mark by the face and kissed him as he remained on one knee. After a minute, Heather went into nurse mode, "Now, get up off this floor."

"Baby, I'm fine. I've been practicing this for a while now."

"Oh, you have?"

"You thought that while you were out shopping I been laying around in bed?"

"Well, yea."

"Nah. I've been doing all of this so that I could

surprise you. That nurse did her damn thing."

"I never really took you for such a romantic." Heather confessed.

"Well, there are a lot of things you'll learn about me. We are still just beginning."

"Oh, my. What have I just gotten myself into?"

"You have no idea, my love."

Mark rose up from the floor and joined Heather back on the bed. He was still moving slow, but all of his parts were seeming to function just fine. Heather saw his erection peek through the robe.

"Hmmm, you've been holding out on me."

"I have." Mark kissed Heather deeply, sucking seductively on her lips.

"I should spank you for being such a bad boy."

"Then you'd better get to it. I've been very bad."

Heather untied the robe and revealed Mark's lean muscular chest and naked body. Heather caressed the scar on his right love handle.

"You are in so much trouble." Heather grabbed

his erect penis and stroked it.

"You know that's my spot, babe."

"Oh, really? And I am going to enjoy making you squirm."

Mark laid on the bed and Heather rubbed all over his chest, down his happy trail.

"Are you ready for this?" She asked.

"Hell, yeah. It's been too long. If I don't bust this nut, I'm going to go crazy. Now get your ass up here." Mark tugged on Heather's t-shirt.

Heather took off her tee and lifted her mini skirt.

"No, take all of it off. I've waited too long and I want to see all of you.

Heather got off the bed and stepped out of her skirt. Mark looked mesmerized. His eyes watched her every move. His penis was still erect and waiting. Heather was naked except for the diamond ring that glittered from her finger. She got on the bed ready to mount her man when a there was a bang on the door.

"What the fuck!" Mark yelled.

"It's Brandon! Something's happened. I need to talk to you."

Heather gave Mark a look. "You better talk to him."

Mark looked down at his already limp penis and said, "Shit! I might as well."

"I'll be in the bathroom." Heather said grabbing her cellphone from the nightstand.

"This ain't over!" Mark closed his robe, "Come in." Mark yelled back.

Just before Manny walked in, Heather flashed Mark with her perky breast and pussy just before she closed the bathroom door. Mark looked at Heather and shook his head and smiled.

Heather smiled behind the closed door and held her hand out in front of her and snapped a picture. She tried to think about when he'd have time to get the ring, but that didn't matter. She had him, the man she'd dreamed about. The man she wrote about in so many articles. She started a shower. When the water hit her face, she instantly thought that this moment was too good to be true. In the next moment, she was scared of what all this meant. She would be instantly thrust into the spotlight and ridiculed by everyone who was jealous of Mark or of her. The role of staying behind the scenes was over.

CHAPTER EIGHT

"What!" Justice nearly screamed.

"You heard me!" Heather nearly screamed back.

"But wait. I thought you guys were just friends."

"We are. Things have changed since we moved in together and we've spent so much time together." Heather emphasized.

"I mean, when did you fall in love with him?" Justice was curious.

"Jus, what kind of question is that?" Heather hissed.

"It's different than being a fan and a lover."

Justice said.

"I know that. I've been in love with him since as long as I can remember."

"As a fan, but now as a person."

"Why are you asking me all of these questions? I thought you would just be happy for me."

"Heather, you know that's not it. I just want you to be sure about what you're about to do. I've known you your whole life. I know you've loved Mark B. since he became Mark B. I know this is a dream come true."

"Then what is the problem?" Heather interjected.

"The problem is...I don't want you to get hurt falling for a celebrity. It's different when you were just working together and playing around, but this is real and celebrity marriages have high divorce rates."

"Got dammit Justice. Are you jealous?"

"Jealous? No, I'm not jealous."

"Then just be happy for me. That's all I need. I don't need you to point out any flaws in my fantasy right now."

"Okay. I'm sorry. I just thought I could be honest with you. You know me, Heather. I don't hold my tongue. Be happy, but be…"

"No buts! Just leave it alone."

"Fine. When is *this* wedding date?"

"We haven't set the date. He just asked me two seconds ago."

Heather had grown irritated with her friend and quickly ended the conversation as soon as Mark opened the bathroom door.

"Is everything okay, baby? You sound upset." Mark asked.

"I just told Justice about my news, but she sounded so jealous."

Heather got up from the edge of the tub and walked passed Mark into the bedroom. Heather sat on top of the bed in Indian style. Mark slowly returned to the bed and sat next to her. He took her by the hand and kissed her ring.

"You may lose some of your friends, baby. People are going to change. Are you going to be able to handle that?"

"She's my best friend, I want her to be happy for me."

"She is. It's just she is probably telling you that have to be careful, blah, blah, blah."

"How do you know?" Heather asked.

"Because, if I were her, I would say the same thing. Just give her some time to warm up to where we are." He smiled and pinched her cheek.

"So what happened with Manny?" Heather changed the subject.

"It's what I already knew. He just found out his brother was arrested for the shooting at the club. He's trying to get him a good lawyer. I told him it's going to be hard to find one that we know from around the way since he just shot and killed one in cold blood."

"What is he going to do?" Heather was concerned.

"I am going to let him handle it. It's his family business, but Manny knows I have his back. I ain't putting no money down on Brandon's ass though. He's the reason I had to spend the last month laying up in bed."

"He's innocent until proven guilty." Heather was optimistic.

"Yea, okay. Well, I trust the source. They say they have a smoking gun."

"I just hope Manny is okay." Heather said.

"He'll be alright. He mentioned some bad luck around him. I didn't know what he was talking about, but he seems to think that his luck is changing."

"Oh no. The man from the grocery store. Manny must think he put a curse on him."

"A curse. What the hell?" Mark jerked his neck

back in disbelief.

"It was that day he came back home all spooked out." Heather explained.

"Oh, yea, I remember that. Manny can be a little spiritual sometime. I hope he shakes this off, though."

"Me, too."

"Now, enough about our best friends. Where were we?" Mark rubbed on Heather's thigh.

"I was naked and about to climb up on top of you and…" Heather started in a seductive voice.

"Oh, yea. That is *exactly* where we were."

Mark took off his robe, climbed up in bed in the same position he was before. Taking Heather's hand, he guided her onto his erect penis. They had not had sex since they agreed to be friend. The shooting incident changed everything. Their bond was stronger than ever. Their feelings grew deeper. They slept in the same bed many times and they never crossed the line, until now.

Heather moaned when she sat on Mark's firm penis. She remembered how he felt, the size, and the penetration. Mark grabbed Heather's waist, he guided her as best he could. Heather leaned forward and rubbed her clit against the foundation of his manhood. Slow strokes were what the doctor ordered. Time was oblivious and unaccounted for. Mark made love to Heather as if it were his first. She felt his love in every stroke and moan. Mark was holding on tight when he was near his orgasm. "Baby...I am going to come."

"I want to come, too."

"Then come with me."

The words serenaded the room. It was like words to a song. Mark and Heather reached their peak together. Mark grabbed Heather's hands and locked them while she rode his penis until all of their energy was depleted. Heather laid forward on Mark's chest with him still deep inside her. She whispered, "You are my dream come true."

By the next month, Mark claimed he was fully recovered and Heather was right on his heels to make sure. He had her in and out of meetings and preparing for the new film project and the wedding all at once. The wedding was a lot of work even with a wedding planner.

Paparazzi were all over the story, but Heather took it all in stride. She knew how to handle them. Even Justice was starting to come around. Heather's family was excited that she finally found a man. They didn't seem to be all that impressed that it was Mark B though. As long as he treated her right was all that mattered.

Heather and Mark were attached at the hip. Everyone, especially them, were over the idea that they were something to gossip about. It took nearly a month to decide on a date.

"Are you ready for this next roller coaster?"

Mark asked Heather as they pulled up to the film studio.

"Which one is that? I feel like I've been on one since we met."

"Is that so?"

"Kinda. I mean, nothing is the way I expected."

"Is that a bad thing?"

"It's just been surreal."

"Tell me about that." Mark looked eager to hear.

"Maybe on our wedding night." Heather teased and kissed Mark on the cheek just as Manny opened her door.

"Oh, hell nah!" Mark laughed at the perfect timing.

"What's up boss?" Manny peeked in as Heather hopped out of the SUV.

"Stop that woman. She's been holding out on me." Mark teased.

Manny looked behind his shoulder and Heather was already two steps ahead. Mark slid out of the truck slowly and trotted up to catch her. A nice pat on the ass got her attention.

"Ahh!" Heather squealed.

"Don't leave me hanging next time." Mark said and grabbed Heather's arm and put it in his.

Heather squeezed his muscular bicep as they walked in to the studio together. It was an organized chaotic place. People walking around, the actors were waiting in the lobby, and The B-Side, the production name Heather came up with, was behind a clear glass wall. When Mark and Heather walked in, the team stood up to greet them.

"Hello everyone." Mark said.

They all spoke at once to greet the couple. Mark sat at the head of the table and Heather sat on his right. They talked about the casting that was about to take place and Mark's expectations. Once he set the tone he said, "Let's do this."

Mark adjourned the meeting and the staff exited toward the audition studio. Mark held Heather back for a quick minute.

He looked her in the eyes, "Take notes. This is a new project and I don't want to miss a beat. I know you'll pick up on things they may miss. We're in this together."

"Yes, we are. I got you babe. Don't worry." Heather assured him.

"Good," Mark kissed his fiancé on her red matte lips as he opened the door to exit, "and did I tell you how sexy you look today?"

"Yes."

"When?" Mark raised an eyebrow.

"Just now." Heather said and kissed him right back as she walked through the door with her crisp white blouse and black skinny slacks and red patent leather heels.

"Hmmm! That woman!" Mark groaned.

♠♠♠

On the way back from the casting, Mark received a call. "Hello. Hello?"

"He missed." The voice said.

"Who is this?" Mark said angrily.

The phone went dead.

Heather looked at Mark for an explanation.

"I don't know who that was. I have to get a new number. Someone is playing games."

"I'll call the phone company when we get back to the condo."

"Thanks baby. I hate doing that all the time. These crazy fans get my number and play games."

The phone rang again.

"Hello."

"He missed the mark, Mark." The auto-tune voice said.

"Who missed the mark?! What are you talking

about?!" Mark questioned loudly.

Manny looked through the rearview at Heather and slowed down the vehicle.

"Next time we won't miss." The voice said.

The phone went dead again.

"What the fuck?" Mark said looking at the phone.

"What?" Manny said as he was now pulled over to the side of the highway.

"They talking about they missed the mark and that they won't miss next time. What the fuck are they talking about?" Mark was agitated.

"Do you think that it may have something to do with the shooting?" Manny asked.

Heather didn't say anything. She sat still because she could see the anger in Mark's eyes. All she could think about was what he just said. Did someone miss? Who was the target if Darrin wasn't it? Was Mark supposed to be dead or was she the target?

"I don't know, but I have a few calls to make. Your brother better not be behind this shit."

"Brandon didn't do this. I can't believe he would shoot up a club like that. I think he's being set up."

"Let's go. Get me back to the condo. Matter of fact, I need to go back to New York. I need to see some people face to face."

The ride was eerily quiet for the rest of the way. Heather was thinking about what Mark had to do back in New York that he couldn't do in L.A. There was no way she was going to ask. This was starting to feel like a drama movie all over again and she did not want any parts of it, but unfortunately, she was already a part of it. This was the life she agreed to when she said she would marry Mark B. James, one of the most popular hip hop artists in the world. Someone was always plotting, scheming to get him caught up in something.

Back at the condo, Mark started packing his suitcase. Heather sat at the computer booking the jet for a red eye flight to LaGuardia. When she finished, she turned around and watched Mark fold his things and put them in a bag.

"What bag are you taking, babe?" Mark asked.

"Bag?" Heather was confused.

"Yes, bag. You need to pack for a couple days."

"Mark, I didn't know I was going with you. I only booked one seat." Heather was matter of fact.

"Well then you need to change it. I am not leaving you here with some maniac running around making threats."

Heather didn't think of it like that. After he made that statement, it dawned on her that she probably wouldn't feel safe if he wasn't around anyway.

"Okay. I just thought that you were going by yourself."

"I would feel better if you were with me. I will handle my business when I get there, but at least you won't be over 3000 miles away."

"Alright, alright. I'll pack."

"I should spank you for even thinking you had an option." Mark laughed and pulled Heather up from the desk.

"Spank away!"

Mark did spank Heather on the ass one good time and she was off getting her carry-on sized bag from the walk-in closet. When she walked away, Mark sat on the edge of the bed and watched her. Heather turned back and saw him. It was something in his eyes, she didn't know what it was, but he looked different. Heather couldn't quite put her finger on what was going through his head and based on the recent events, she wasn't sure if she even wanted to know.

Later that night, they boarded the private jet. Manny stayed back at the condo; which was quite unusual. Mark and Manny were typically each other's shadow, but when Heather changed the flight to put herself on it, she made sure to ask about Manny. Mark was explicitly clear that Manny was not tagging along on this trip.

Heather found her way back into the sleeping room on the jet. It was going to be a long flight and they had the jet all to themselves. Mark stayed in the main cabin on his laptop. Heather didn't ask what he was up to and he didn't say. She let him take care of business. There was something pressing on his mind, she could sense it.

What had seemed like a full night rest only took several hours. Mark came into the room and nudged Heather to wake up.

"We're about to land." He said.

Heather made her way into the main cabin to get her seat belt on. Within minutes they landed.

The limousine was waiting to pick them up from the runway. When they got inside, Heather noticed Mark's distance.

"Is everything OK?" Heather asked.

"I just have a lot on my mind. That call got me asking a lot of questions and I won't be cool until I go talk to one of my peoples from around the way." Mark assured her.

"I can go stay with Justice if you want."

"No. I don't want anyone to even know you are here with me. I booked us at the Waldolf in Manhattan."

"Okay. I have some writing to do anyway."

"Good. I won't be long. I just want to find out what the fuck is going on with these calls and threats."

"I understand." Heather didn't really understand, but she had to play along.

"Thank you, babe. Don't worry. I got this under control."

"I am sure you do." Heather was hesitant to say those words, but she had to. She had to make Mark believe that she was calm and that he had things under control, even though he didn't look like it.

When they arrived at the hotel, Mark had everything already arranged. He must have spent his time on the flight planning. The suite was just as nice as their condo. Heather felt right at home.

"I hope this is okay." Mark said.

"Of course, it is."

"I'll be back as soon as I can. Did you program my new number?"

"Yes, baby. I have the new number."

"Good. Call me if you need anything."

Mark made sure that everything was in order before he left. He dropped off his bag in the bedroom. He changed into something that helped him blend in. Heather raised an eyebrow as she watched Mark transform into a less than regular looking guy.

"I am still Mark B. from the hood and don't you ever forget it." Mark said popping his collar and putting on a baseball cap. He leaned over to kiss Heather on the lips before leaving and just like that he was gone and she was alone.

♠♠♠

Hours later, there is a knock on the door. She ignored the knock. Seconds later, the knock got harder and faster. This time Heather got up and went to the door to look out the peephole.

The person on the outside of the door looked like a hotel worker, so Heather opened the door.

"Can I help…" She started before she was shoved inside the room and knocked over the head with the butt of a gun.

Her face laying flat on the floor, Heather was still conscious. Her vision was blurry. She could see the feet of someone walking around the room. She couldn't move even if she tried. She felt weak. Her eyes closed slowly.

When Heather finally opened her eyes, she was afraid to get up. She didn't know if the person was still in the room or not. She waited and listened for sounds. It was deathly quiet. She sat up on the floor and looked around the room. No one was there.

Heather went to her purse for her cellphone, but it was gone. She picked up the hotel phone to call Mark when she realized her engagement ring was not on her finger. "Oh, no!" she said then heard the recording on the line.

"The number you have reached has been disconnected." The operator said.

"Shit!" Heather forgot that she just changed Mark's number and she had not memorized the new one yet. She tried to recall from memory, but she couldn't. The only number she could remember was Justice's. She had the same number since they were in college.

"Justice speaking."

"Jus, it's me."

"Heather. What the hell are you doing calling me from Manhattan."

"I can't tell you that right now. Can you come to the Waldolf?"

"When?"

"Now."

"Now? What's going on?"

"Just come and I will tell you as soon as you get here. And don't tell anyone that you're coming to see me."

"Heather...what the hell is going on? You're starting to scare me."

"Please. I just need you to come. Now."

"I'm on my way."

"Thanks, sis."

After giving Justice the hotel room number,

Heather went into the bathroom and looked at her head. It was throbbing. She had a small bruise where she was hit in the temple by the gun. After she realized that it was not that bad, she went into the room and checked for any other things that may have been stolen. Mark's bag was rummaged through and so was Heather's. All she could think about was the phone calls and the fact that Mark was still gone. She didn't even know how long she was out.

Thirty minutes later, a knock at the door startled Heather. She ran over and peeked through the hole and saw that it was Justice.

"Come in." Heather grabbed her friend by the hand and slammed the door.

"Ouch! What the hell, Heather."

"Sorry, I just had to get you inside quick. I don't know who else is out there."

"Who else would be out there? And why are you in the city and didn't tell me?"

"Sit down. I have to tell you what's been going on."

Justice was about to sit down until she seen the bruise. "What the hell happened to you? Is Mark beating you?" Justice came closer and looked at the bump.

"No! It's nothing like that."

"That's what it looks like to me, so you better get to explaining before I make some calls to handle his ass."

"Look, sit down. I'll explain everything."

Justice sat down on the sofa inside the living room of the suite. Heather told her everything that she had found out about the shooting that killed her fiancé, including the crazy stalker that blew black dust on Manny in L.A.

"Why haven't you told me any of this, sis?" Justice was concerned.

"I didn't want to worry you and I still don't know what this is all about." Heather said.

"What is Mark up to?"

"I don't know. He's been gone for hours and he's going to be pissed that I opened the door and someone came in the room and stole my engagement ring. I am just scared. You're the only person that I could call."

"It's okay. I'll wait with you until he comes back."

Mark always felt like Brooklyn was still home, but the streets did not feel as welcoming as they used to. He passed street hustlers, prostitutes, and homeless people that were staples on the corners and under the subway bridges. The reason he decided to start his music career was to get out of the hood. The return to these streets was always with a purpose. To hear the streets talk, you had to come listen for yourself.

Mark drove down Fulton Street and pulled into

his homeboy's auto shop parking lot. When he got out the rental car he walked through the parking lot unnoticed as expected. New Yorkers were not the friendliest and looking people in the face was not something they did. Mark made sure he wore what a regular dude on the street would wear so no one would notice him.

Mark walked into the garage and found his friend rolling out from under an old Model T.

"What's up B!" Henry St. Germaine said surprised.

"Whad'up!" Mark said giving Henry a hand to stand up.

"What are you doing all the way in these gutters?" Henry said wiping his hands on his carpenter pants.

"You know why I am here, don't even trip."

"Ya' I know. I am glad to see you aight. These mutha'fuckas grimy out here. I got some information for you. They trying to handle you on some petty shit." Henry explained.

"I don't even know what the issue is and I am usually up on that."

"That's because you too caught up in that chic you with. You know she's the reason behind all yo drama."

"What? What does she have to do with Darrin getting shot. That was her best friend's dude." Mark explained.

"Yeah, well apparently, that older chic you had working for you got beef with you and she hired someone to take care of the problem."

Mark's temperature started to rise, "Gabrielle Oni is behind this. I don't understand."

"Well you betta get to understanding. That crooked ass attorney was a whole'notha situation and his girl...that anchor broad, yeah, she ain't too clean either. She got some real low key ties to the streets from what I hear. Her boy was doing some dirty shit on the underground scene so that shit was outta her hands."

"Damn, I been out the loop." Mark said.

Henry went into his office and Mark followed him and they both sat down. Behind closed doors Henry gave Mark the rundown on the underground black market that had a lot of key professional players.

"Man, you have been valuable as always. You know I owe you for this." Mark gave Henry dap.

"You know you my people and I don't want to see you caught up. You left the streets and I respect that. You and your girl deserve to be happy away from all this shit. So, just know you ain't just dealing with no jealous broad...you marked. You dealing with some street hugs that don't give a fuck about your life, career or your girl. They trying to knock you down so they can get paid."

"Oh, I hear you, loud and clear."

"Let me know if you need anything else." Henry offered.

"As a matter of fact. I do. Set up a meeting."

Mark pulled a thick yellow envelop out of his pocket and slid it across the table to Henry. Henry took the envelop and put it inside his carpenter jumpsuit. Mark didn't say another word. He gave Henry some dap and was out.

♠♠♠

It felt like forever, but Mark came bursting into the room. "Heather!"

"I'm in here." Heather said from the living room.

"What the fuck happened? I called your phone and some dude picked up and said you were dead."

"Dead?" Heather questioned.

"How did he get your phone and what the hell is she doing here?"

"I am her best friend and she called me asshole! Where have you been?"

"None of your got damn business! Heather, what's going on?"

Heather watched her two favorite people go at each other and she sulked.

"I'm sorry, baby...what's going on...what happened?" Mark tried to calm down.

Heather told Mark what happened, even about the ring. He rubbed Heather's forehead. He kissed it as she sobbed.

"Don't cry, we're going to be alright. I will get you another ring. You have to trust me."

"Trust you? My girl has been involved in more drama since the day she met your ass. I think it's time for her to take a break from you until all of this shit is sorted out."

"Get the fuck out! I got this!" Mark yelled.

"Justice!" Heather interjected.

"Heather, I think you should go back to Atlanta with your parents for a while until this blows over." Justice suggested.

"I am not leaving him. I don't want to go to Atlanta." Heather demanded.

"I happen to agree with Justice on this." Mark lied.

He did not trust Justice, but he could not let her or Heather know that he was privy to some street knowledge. He continued to support Justice's idea.

"It's not up for discussion. You're going to catch a flight out of NYC in the morning. Thanks Justice for being here with her. I got it from here." Mark assured her.

"You better. I will kill your ass if something happens to my sister."

"And you should, but let's not talk like that. I got enough to worry about. I don't need you on my ass, too." Mark said seriously.

Justice said her goodbyes and was gone. Mark turned to Heather and said, "I can't fix this problem above the law, so I have to send you away to keep you out of it."

"I don't even want to know what you mean by all of that. I just want this to end so we can finish planning our life together."

"We will. You can work on the wedding plans while you're in Atlanta. Will that make you feel better?"

"No."

"Why not?" Mark asked.

"I am going to be worried about you. That's why."

"Don't worry." Mark pleaded.

"Well did you find out who was behind all of this."

"Yes, but I can't tell you what I know just yet."

"Why not?"

"I need to keep you innocent. I can't risk you knowing information that may be used against me."

"What are you saying?"

"The person who was the target that night was

not just Darrin. It was us, too."

"What? Why?"

"That is the part that I can't tell you. If I tell you, then you will know too much. Besides, whomever came into this room was here to send a message. If they wanted to finish the job, then they would have."

"I am a target because I am with you." Heather stated.

"People don't always like the decisions that I make. Sometimes they try to seek revenge. This will be over in a couple days. Now, let's go. We're leaving this hotel."

Mark grabbed his things and Heather grabbed hers. She had not even unpacked, but the intruder had tossed her things on the floor while searching her bag.

"I need a new cell phone." Heather said as they were walking out of the hotel.

"I got you."

"Baby, just put me up in another hotel. I don't want to go back to Atlanta." Heather fussed all the way out of the room.

As they walked down the hall, Mark looked back and made sure there was no one following them.

When they entered the elevator, "I am not sending you no damn where. You are going to be here with me. I just said those things because I think the room was bugged."

"Bugged. By whom?"

"I don't know who this bitch has working for her."

"Her?"

"This is about some female?"

"I will tell you when we get in car."

Inside the car, Heather put on her seat belt. She'd never been in the car with Mark driving before. This was about to be an adventure.

"Mark, who knew that we were at this hotel?"

Heather started an inquiry of questions to find answers.

"The only person that would know anything is Manny."

"Would he tell anyone?"

"I can't say right now. It's hard to put my finger on who is all behind this shit."

"Manny wouldn't betray you." Heather defended him.

"I thought that about his brother, but that bitch ass nigga was the damn shooter at the club. The club scene knows Brandon used to work for me so maybe they thought it was cool to just let him in. When they swept the place there was a video of Brandon going into the bathroom and coming out with a different shirt and a mask. I did not even know he was at the party, cause I sure as hell didn't invite him. By the time he started shooting, everyone scattered the place and he took off his mask and ran out with the crowd."

"What do I have to do with it?"

"You're close to me and the person who wants to hurt me wants to hurt you, too."

"Why? What have I done?"

"You stole me from her."

"Her? Who?" Heather asked.

"Gabriella."

"Ms. Oni."

Mark nodded his head as he turned on 7th Avenue headed uptown. He was not going to tell her anything about Justice's ties because he didn't have proof that she was behind his shooting. She was connected, he just didn't know how. So, he had to keep the focus on Gabriella.

CHAPTER NINE

Heather tried not to make her anger known because she did not want to alarm Mark, but it was obvious that her silence was as loud as any cussing and fussing that she could ever do.

"What?" Mark finally broke the silence.

"I don't think I should say what I am thinking."

"No, that is exactly what you should say."

"So, why is she so obsessed with you that she is doing all of this?"

"I don't know that yet." Mark lied. He had to

pretend he did not know the full story behind the problem. Protecting Heather was his priority.

"Why not? You said you never did anything with her, so why is she acting like a woman scorned?"

"I am trying to figure all of that out. What is boggling to me is the fact that Brandon is involved. They couldn't stand each other."

"But neither of them work for you anymore." Heather said.

"That's true, but Brandon and I did not part on bad terms, so this is not adding up."

"I guess that doesn't matter." Heather said.

"I promise you baby, me and Gabrielle, I mean, Ms. Oni never had a thing."

"Did she want it to be a thing?"

"Yea, badly, but that was when we first started working together. After I put her in her place, she backed off or at least I thought she did."

"How? What happened? Tell me everything."

Heather demanded the whole store.

Mark told Heather about the time that Ms. Oni tried to seduce him after a show. It was not the first time, but when she tried to stay in his suite, he had to tell her no. Manny had to escort her to her room and book her on a separate flight the next day.

"Why didn't you fire her then?" Heather asked as she looked out the window of the city she still loved.

"She was so damn good at her job. Besides that, I was tired of going through different people. She caught on fast and I didn't have to hold her hand."

"Why does she want to hurt me?"

"You're the reason she believes I fired her."

"Well, am I?"

"I can't lie to you, babe. Yes. I started seeing the red flags when I didn't hire her recommendation and she was really pissed at how you tried to check her...I mean us, at the first meeting."

"But I had nothing to do with your hiring decision. For all I knew, I was chosen by Musiq, not you."

"She tried to discredit your career and dig up things from your past to prove that you were just another groupie."

"But you know that stuff is not true."

"I know. That is when I said she had to go. I wanted you from that first day I met you. On the road she saw me with a few chicks, but no one serious. When she saw how I welcomed you into the fold, she felt threatened."

Heather did not want to know any more about Ms. Oni. She was disgusted with the fact that she was trying to hurt her over some crush she had with her boss. Heather also had to believe Mark was telling the truth about not leading her on. He was a little too friendly at times and she could have taken it the wrong way.

The rest of the ride was filled with the sounds of smooth jazz. Mark turned up the volume and put his hand on Heather's thigh. They felt like a normal couple driving through New York City; something that had not happened since they started dating.

When they pulled up to a brownstone, Mark punched buttons on the keypad to open the garage. He pulled in and Heather looked at him dumbfounded.

"I thought we were going to a hotel."

"I changed my mind. If someone is going to try and get to you again, they'll have to go through my Aunt Mae."

"Your Aunt Mae?"

"Yes. She raised me after my mom passed when I was a kid."

"Okay. I wasn't prepared to meet your family under these circumstances."

"Well, this is where I should have brought you

in the first place. No one messes with my Aunt Mae. She'll shot first and ask questions later."

"Oh, lord."

"Don't worry. We'll be back to our wedding planning soon enough." Mark kissed his fiancé's cheek before turning off the ignition.

"We have a conference call today for the film. Are you going to be on it?" Heather asked.

"You handle it babe. I have to go take care of some things."

"You're leaving me again?" Heather pouted.

"I won't be long, I promise." Mark said and opened the car door.

When they got out of the car, Aunt Mae appeared in the doorway.

"Markie!" she yelled.

Mark hugged his Aunt Mae and turned to introduce Heather.

"Auntie, this is my fiancé, Heather."

"Fiancé? You ain't tell me about no fiancé.

Come'er girl and give your Auntie Mae a hug."

Mark's Aunt Mae was born in the south and moved up to NYC in the late 80s just before her sister passed. Mark's grandfather was a rolling stone and when he was ready to settle down, he chose Mark's grandmother Florence who was born and raised in Harlem. Mark's mother Vivien never knew she had a sister until she got older. Mark's grandfather introduced Vivien and Mae when they were in their teens and they stayed in touch. A few years before his mother died, Mae moved to New York to be closer to the only sister she had. Mae never had any children of her own so adopting Mark when her sister passed was a blessing. Her southern accent and hospitality was still the same as it was back then.

Heather felt right at home with Aunt Mae. Mark left to handle his business and she took the conference call about the film project. Business as usual.

Mark pulled into a New York City dingy alley. If the allies could talk, they would tell of all the unmentionable crimes that the cities never see. His rental was incognito enough to fit in, but it didn't have tinted windows; which he was not used to. He stopped at the door marked, STINGER. Mark recognized the location as an old after hours spot from back in the day. New York was notorious for using allies as entryways into low key spots.

Mark got out the car and knocked on the door. When it opened, he saw an oversized black man with a crazy crooked eye. He motioned for Mark to follow him down a dimly lit hallway. He entered a room and could not believe his eyes.

"What the fuck are you doing here?!"

Heather had to use the landline to check her voicemail to see if she'd missed any calls. She was going through serious withdrawals without her cellphone.

"Manny, what's up?" Heather called Manny back.

"Where's Mark?" He asked.

"I don't know where he is. Why?" Heather was honest.

"I need to talk to him and he's not answering his phone." Manny sounded urgent.

"What is it Manny? You're scaring me." Heather sat up in the chair and listened attentively.

"This situation is bigger than what he knows. There are some big players trying to get involved in bringing him down."

"Manny, this isn't about anyone trying to bring him down. What are you talking about?"

"Trust me. They have him believing it has to

do with that bitch Gabriella, but it's more than that."

Heather didn't say anything. She listened to the concern in Manny's voice.

"Mark is being set up for another hit. I need to find him." Manny continued.

"I don't know where he is. He told me to sit tight and wait for him."

"Where are you?" Manny asked.

Heather was quiet. She remembered the incident that just happened at the hotel and how Mark moved her to a safer place where no one would look and apparently Aunt Mae did not have Wi-Fi. She was literally disconnected from the world with no cellphone or internet.

"Heather, where are you?"

"I can't tell you."

"Why not?" Manny chuckled.

"It's just a lot going on and Mark doesn't want anyone knowing where I am."

"But this is me." Manny sounded rejected.

"I know, but…"

"But, what? You know I would never do anything to hurt you. You guys are my family. I can't believe what I am hearing."

"I'm sorry."

"Don't be sorry. If he doesn't want me knowing where you are, then that is cool. Tell Mark I said he needs to call me as soon as he gets back."

"Okay." Heather said and the phone went dead.

Heather cradled Aunt Mae's old school phone in her hand for a few minutes thinking about what Manny said. She didn't know who to trust at this point and it wasn't going to be her fault that someone showed up at Aunt Mae's place. The last thing she needed was for Mark to distrust her.

Heather tried to focus on business, but it was hard. Their first film shoot was coming up in a few days and here she was held captive on the lower level of a brownstone in the middle of Harlem. Her thoughts went back to the desk job she had at the magazine a year ago. Life was normal and quite uneventful until she took the job as a tour journalist. What felt like a career opportunity of a lifetime has become a life long decision alright, and her career has taken a backseat to all of it. In that moment, Heather became angry. What was happening to her life? It didn't feel like hers anymore. She felt trapped and consumed by the life of Mark B. James. How was she supposed to focus with all of this drama going on? She had to do something to change this or she would drive herself insanely mad. Heather took out her laptop from her bag and started writing.

"Heather," Mark whispered.

Heather was curled up on the couch with her

hand tucked under a pillow. "Hmmm?"

"Wake up." Mark said.

"What's going on?"

"We've got to go. We're going back to LA."

"Now?" Heather tried to check the time on the nightstand, but realized that she wasn't at home and there was no clock there to look at.

"Yes, now. We have the jet set. We need to get going."

"Okay. I need to grab my things."

"I have all of your things and I told Aunt Mae that we're heading out."

"We need to talk." Heather mumbled.

"On the way. I promise." Mark pulled Heather up and helped her into her shoes.

It felt like they were in a rush, but Heather didn't say anything. She had a plan and when they got back to LA, she planned to tell Mark about it.

On the ride to the airport, Heather decided not to talk. Things felt eerie and probably better left unsaid. At this point, she didn't know what he was doing or up to to fix this "problem". Whether Manny was right about what he said or not, Heather had her own solution.

"Are you ready to talk?" Mark asked from the back of the limo.

"Nah. I'll wait. I don't know what kind of company we're keeping these days. By the way, Manny called while you were out." Heather looked toward the strange man driving the limo. Since she and Mark met, Manny was the only driver she knew.

"He's my driver, Winston. He's also my uncle, my Aunt Mae's ex-husband. You can talk. What's on your mind?" Mark explained.

Heather spilled the beans. "This is too much for me, Mark. This life and all of this hiding out. I am not cut out for this." Heather wanted to wait until they got back to LA, but the door was open. Mark's face was sulking.

"I can't…" Heather started, but Mark interrupted.

"I know. You can't do this." He accepted what she said and faced the busy streets as they drove through Harlem. Heather turned to look out the other side. It was silent for the remainder of the drive to the airport.

CHAPTER TEN

"Cut! That's a wrap. Great job everyone." Mark B. shouted to the crew. Those were the famous words to close out a successful production.

Back in LA, Heather and Mark started filming nonstop until they finished the project. It was the glue they couldn't unglue. Heather didn't ask any more questions about the situation and Mark didn't offer updates. Heather didn't move out because Mark wouldn't hear of it. She moved into the spare room down the hall. They literally became roommates again.

"Lunch?" Mark offered.

"Nah. I have a column to write for Prime Time."

"You picked up another job?"

"Yes. I figured I'll need to get my own place soon."

"Ah, I see." Mark tried to seem unmoved.

"I'll see you back at the condo. I have some things to wrap up here." Heather walked away.

Her heart was still hurting over the decision to break up and although it had only been two months, she had to admit that the anxiety she felt was starting to subside. Heather was beginning to feel as if life was heading back to normal.

♠♠♠

Inside one of her favorite restaurants while writing her column, Heather noticed a couple of people snickering at her. Life wasn't all the way normal and it probably wouldn't be for a while. One bold person decided to come to her table and sit down.

"Excuse me, I was wondering if you could do me a favor." The strange young person asked.

"I'm sorry, but who are you?"

"Oh, my bad. I'm Young Pirate and I have this mixtape that I want to give Mark B. Can you get it to him for me?"

"Ah, I guess."

"Ain't you his fiancé and shit?"

"Ahhhh," Heather wasn't sure if she should answer that one. Rumors had not got out about their engagement being off and she wanted to keep it that way, "Yea. I will give him the CD. Put your contact info on the front."

"It's already on there." The young rapper pointed to the bad penmanship written on the front of the cd.

"Got it." Heather nodded and put the cd in her

bag.

"Thanks lady."

"You're welcome." Him not knowing her name was probably a good thing.

The rapper got up from the table and went back over to his friends. They tried not to stare the rest of the time, but it was unavoidable. Heather started to pack her things to leave. Her privacy and concentration was gone. On the way out Heather bumped into a man, "Excuse me." She said. When she looked up it was the creepy man from the grocery store. The voodoo man.

Heather rushed through the door and hailed the first cab she saw. When inside, she looked back at the restaurant exit and the man was standing outside watching her. He wore all black, his hair was jet black and he had deep dark eyes. Who was that guy? Heather pulled out her camera in the moment and snapped a picture. The cab pulled off from the curb and into traffic.

When she was inside the condo, she pulled out her cellphone to look at the picture and the image was unrecognizable. The background was crystal clear, but the man's image was very blurry. "What the hell?"

"What the hell, what?" Mark came from the kitchen with a bottled water, a sandwich and no shirt.

Heather was thrown off by his bare chest, but she showed him the picture. "Who is that?" He asked trying to make out the image.

"It's the voodoo man that Manny and I seen at the grocery store a while back." Heather explained.

"You saw him again? Why is it so blurry?" Mark asked.

"That's what so weird. Look, see the people in the background? They are clear. I don't know what happened."

Heather went into her bag for the cd and dropped her phone inside in its place. "Here, this is from Young Pirate." She handed Mark the cd.

"Young who? Someone recognized you?"

"Of course, they did. I don't think they will ever forget us."

"They don't have to. We're still very close, Heather."

"I know. Speaking of close, where's Manny. I want to show him this picture." Heather wanted to change the topic.

"Manny's not going to be here with us anymore. I've hired someone else." Mark said.

"What? When? Why?" Heather sounded disappointed.

"I have my reasons, Heather."

"What reasons? Aside from you, he was the only other person in this game that I trusted. What happened, Mark?" Heather insisted.

"I couldn't trust him. He was the only person who knew you were at that hotel. He said he didn't tell anyone, but at this point, things aren't adding up to where I am comfortable. I just couldn't trust him. He tried to tell me that I was being set up, but...."

"Was?" Heather questioned.

"Yes, was. This situation is handled."

"Why didn't you tell me?"

"You broke up with me so I just left it alone." Mark concluded.

"I broke it off because I am not cut out for living life on the edge and hiding out. I don't want that type of life, Mark."

"Life with me is not easy, Heather."

"Easy, ha!" Heather tried to give Mark a little thump on his rock solid chest.

Mark grabbed her arm before she could land the shot. He pulled her to him. Heather inhaled and smelled his cologne. He knew it was her favorite when she closed her eyes and exhaled. They didn't speak a word. She tilted her forehead and it met his soft lips. "I'm sorry." Mark said, "I'm sorry." He said again and again.

Heather melted in his arms and still didn't say a word. Mark held Heather to him, "You're the one and I will wait as long as it takes."

Heather was still silent, but she remained in his embrace because she knew she loved him. Mark B. James was her dream guy who was no longer a dream. He was hers, yet she was pushing him away out of fear. She didn't know what to do.

Mark picked her up and put her on the counter. He lifted her skirt and revealed her moist sweet spot. Heather didn't refuse the pleasure. Mark also didn't ask for permission, he kissed the inside of her thigh and made his way to where he wanted to be. With his index finger he grabbed the crotch of her thong and moved it aside. With his thumb, rubbed on her cleanly shaven cookie. His tongue was ready for some sugar as he stroked her perky clit as she moaned.

"Damn, baby, I needed this, so bad." Heather

whispered.

"Shhhhh...." Mark hissed back.

Heather did not say another word. At the point of her climax, Mark entered her with only the tip of his manhood and gave her slow, short strokes. He increased the pace, Heather leaned back on the counter for balance as he draped her legs over his arms for the perfect angle. Mark was nearing his climax, but he held it as he felt Heather's exhilarating muscles pulsate and get wetter and wetter. The strokes got quicker and quicker, but he kept the head in staying at the forefront of her g-spot until she exploded all over his shift, thighs and down to his pants, that had fallen to his ankles. Heather's squirt gushed and gushed with each mini stroke. Mark was drowning in her wetness as joined her climax. He pulled her closer to him, shaft still firmly inside her, legs still dangling from his arms, and kissed her forehead.

"You are amazing." Mark confessed.

"Look what you made me do." Heather said looking down at the puddle they made on the floor.

"Yeah, let me go get something to clean this up, but let me get one more of those showers!" Mark chuckled and penetrated Heather one more time. Mark had discovered another pleasure with the woman he loved. He couldn't pass up the opportunity for more.

The intercom buzzer buzzed as soon as he got his last nut. Mark cursed, took a deep breath and wobbled over to the intercom with pants still at his ankles. "Yes."

"Mr. James, there's for B-Side Productions." The security said.

"From who?"

"It say's Bi-Way Construction."

"Alright, hold it. I will walk down to pick it up shortly."

"Bi-Way Construction?"

"I have been working with a company on a

new construction project, but it's not with Bi-Way. I turned down their proposal weeks ago."

"What new construction?" Heather inquired.

"It's a secret and don't try to badger it out of me." Mark insisted.

"Fine, since you're keeping secrets and all, I don't want to send you the wrong message. I really enjoyed making love to you, but we're not back together." Heather kissed Mark on the lips.

"I said I will wait as long as it takes." Mark said joyfully putting another peck on Heather's lips.

After cleaning the mess from the floor and changing into some dry shorts, Mark left out the door to fetch the package. Heather went into her room and flopped down on the bed face first. She nearly screamed, but kept her composure. Instead she laid quiet and didn't hear anything except the sound of her own heart beating. Then she heard banging! She nearly leaped out of the bed, "What the hell?" She ran down the hall looking for the cause of the noise. Mark was nowhere in sight. Heather began to panic as she looked around the condo. When Heather reached the front entrance, she was almost knocked over by guard as she opened the door.

"Call 9-1-1!" The guard said.

"Where's Mark?" Heather yelled.

"Miss! Call 9-1-1 now!" The guard said before he passed out.

Heather fumbled through her bag for her phone, then called 9-1-1. She ran out the door while on the phone with the operator.

"Yes, I need an ambulance!" Heather said frantically.

"What happened, ma'am?" The operator asked.

"I don't' know. My security told me to call the police just before he passed out." Heather explained as she leaned down to check the guard's pulse, he was still alive. She ran to the security booth.

"Is anyone else hurt?" The operator asked.

"I am looking for my fiancé." Heather said. She rushed down the driveway and saw Mark laid out on the ground near the security booth. Heather dropped the phone and ran over to him.

"Mark!" Heather screamed as she checked for a pulse. "Wake up! Don't you dare do this to me, again!" Heather said as she started to administer CPR.

Moments later, in the faded background Heather heard the ambulance approaching. Mark was not visibly hurt, but he was unconscious and that was what scared Heather the most. She didn't know what happened. She looked around the area and noticed the source.

A piece of tubing that could have visibly contained blueprints was blown off on at the top. She looked around the area for any more clues, but there was nothing. The sirens got closer and closer and within seconds a fire truck and an ambulance came to a screeching halt as they drove right up to the security gate.

The paramedics jumped out of the vehicle and immediately came to Mark's aid. "The guard is by the front door." Heather pointed to the other EMT.

"Is he alive?" The paramedic asked.

"I don't know, I think so. He just passed out." Heather answered, but only focused on Mark.

"Ma'am what happened here?" A policeman said as he walked over to her with a notepad in hand.

"I don't know. I was inside. When I came out to see what happened they both were passed out."

"Did you see anyone out here after it happened?" The officer asked while writing in the pad.

"No. I didn't see anything!"

The paramedic had Mark on the stretcher and

had attached him to oxygen. Seconds later another stretcher came down the driveway with the security guard on it. Heather went into panic mode. She didn't know what to do. She didn't know who else to call in the moment.

"Manny!" Heather screamed.

"What the fuck do you want?"

"Manny! This is Heather. Someone tried to…" Heather started to explain.

"I know who this is and I don't give a damn what happened to that mutha fucker. I tried to warn his ass, but he fired me, so get off my line." Manny hung up the phone.

She called Justice.

"Mark and the guard are hurt and they are being rushed to the hospital."

"Are you okay, were you hurt?"

"I was inside the house. I am OK, but I don't know what happened. I am so scared."

"You have to get yourself back to Atlanta. It's

too much going on with that man right now and if he gets you killed, I'm going to kill him myself."

"I can't leave him like this!"

"You can't stay either. It's too dangerous. Where is Manny?"

"He doesn't work for Mark anymore."

"Since when? What happened?"

"Mark didn't tell me what happened. I am just in the dark about this whole situation."

"Which is exactly why you need to catch the first plane out of there and get your ass back to your family."

"I can't abandon him like this. I love him, I mean we've planned to get married."

"That's just it. You planned. As in past tense. The wedding is off and so is this shame of a relationship."

Heather was hurting and she was not in the mood to argue with Justice. She ran inside to grab her purse and locked the door to the condo. She jumped into the ambulance, just as it was about to leave and watched the medics work to stabilize Mark.

"We're losing him!"

He was flat lining. The ambulance was weaving in and out of traffic before it finally arrived at the ER. They jumped out of the vehicle and rushed him into the hospital. Heather was in a panic and followed them until they closed the door in her face.

A man in a suit came into the waiting area 30 minutes after Heather sat down. He looked at his phone and then over to Heather. "Excuse me. Are you Heather?"

"Who are you?"

"Can I speak to you outside for a second?"

"I can't leave. I need to wait to see what is happening."

"We're just going to be right outside. I just need to talk to you."

"Sorry. I am not leaving. If you want to tell me something, then tell me here." Heather spoke in a louder tone so the people in the waiting room could hear her.

"Fine." The man sat down in the vacant seat next to Heather. He reached into his jacket and pulled out a card.

"Private Investigator, Milestone." Heather read the card.

"Your friend, my friend Justice Swank told me what was going on with you and your rapper boyfriend."

"Well, tell our friend that I do not need a babysitter and he's not my rapper boyfriend." Heather was pissed at his nonchalant statement.

"Look," the agent throws his hands up, "I don't argue with Justice. She's a trusted friend and if she says she needs my help then I don't ask any questions. So you have to deal with it because she obviously cares about you or I wouldn't be here."

"I know you're just here to help, but my patience with my friend is wearing thin. I just want to know what happened. Can you *help* me with that?"

"Well, all I can tell you is that the bomb squad showed up on the scene and they did find the remnants of a poisonous substance on the package. When Mark opened the lid, it expelled the toxins in that immediate area and both Mark and the guard ingested it. Thankfully, it was not opened inside the home or you'd be in there laid out, too."

"What kind of substance was it?"

"It's too early to know. They have to run tests, but they are probably trying to give Mark and the guard some type of antidote that may cover a range of things. Had it been a real explosive, you'd be planning a funeral. Who ever did this want him to suffer really bad or else he'd be dead."

"What should I do?" Heather asked the question she already knew the answer to.

"To be honest, you need to lay low until we get to the bottom of this. I have connections with the local fed office and they will push this under the rug like all of the other unsolved minority casualties."

"I am not leaving LA." Heather persisted.

"I suggest you stay some place safe then until you decide to leave LA. Your condo is a crime scene and it's probably not safe to go back there anyway. Is there anything you need from there? I don't mind stopping by there for you."

"All I want is my laptop and a change of clothes." Heather gave him the key and a list of what to bring.

"Alright. When I come back I expect you to have some accommodations made so I can take you when I get back. I doubt if they let you see him any time soon anyway." Milestone said.

"Thank you."

The PI left the hospital and Heather sat for another hour before she went over to the nurses' station to get an update, but no one was there. A male nurse eventually came to the desk, "May I help you?"

"Yes. I need an update on Mark James." Heather whispered.

"Mark James? The Mark B. James?"

"Yes. He was taken back, but I don't know what's going on."

"Hmmm, let me go find out. I'll be right back."

The nurse left the station and went behind the restricted doors. Heather looked back at the waiting area to see if anyone was staring at her. She tried to be discrete, but that wasn't working when the happy go groupie nurse decided to get loud.

"Ma'am," the nurse peeked through the crack in the restricted door, "come with me."

Heather followed the nurse behind the doors that led down a quiet hallway. The normal hustle and bustle of an ER was not going on in this place. It was quiet and an eerie quiet at that. "Where is everyone?" Heather finally asked.

"We've had to clear the floor." The nurse said.

"Clear the floor. Why?"

"They had to quarantine the area and move your fiancé to a restricted area." The nurse said waving his hands as he talked.

"What happened?"

"I'll have to let the doctors tell you. He's going to make it from what I heard, but they have to keep him in a clean environment for at least 24 hours."

When they arrived at the door there was a police officer standing outside. Heather saw Mark and the security guard sharing a room together. They looked unconscious, but they were both alive. A sigh of relief came over Heather at the sight.

"Did they say what the substance was?" Heather asked the nurse.

"That I don't know either, but I have to say, you're lucky...I mean he's lucky." The nurse said with a chuckle.

"Well thanks for bringing me back here, but if I can't go inside then I'm going to make arrangements to come back."

"Yea, I wasn't supposed to bring you back here, but I wanted you to know he's OK and in good hands. If you like I can call you when he wakes up."

"That would be great."

Heather handed the nurse her business card. He put it inside his smock shirt as he escorted her back to the front of the hospital. When she found her way to the exit she saw the media frenzy. She immediately turned around and pulled out Milestone's card.

"Milestone."

"Hi, it's me, Heather."

"Is everything OK?"

"Please come get me now!"

"What's going on?"

"The entire media franchise is standing outside

this hospital."

"I'm on my way."

Heather went back inside the hospital and did not make eye contact with any one in the waiting area as she passed and went into the restroom.

"Hurry. It's getting kind of weird around here."

"I'll be there in 10 minutes. Just sit tight."

"I'll be in the ladies' room."

When Heather hung up the phone she went inside a stall and stayed there. She didn't like the feeling of being around all of those people. A text message came through from Justice. When Heather opened it, she saw a picture of Mark in the hospital bed.

"What the hell?" Heather spoke aloud. She immediately became furious with the nurse. He must have taken that picture and posted it to social media and like wildfire, it went viral.

"Where did you see this picture?" Heather called Justice.

"It was sent to me. I am working with iGram and FriendBook to get them removed."

"Thanks. I am going to have that nurse's ass!" Heather said.

"Don't worry about it. I am already on it. You just get yourself out of dodge. I understand you've already met Milestone."

"Yes, and he's on his way to pick me up now."

"From where?"

"The hospital."

"Why are you still there?"

"I just found out what happened. I couldn't leave without knowing what happened to Mark. He will be out of it for another 24 hours. They said it was something poisonous."

"What is really going on?" Justice asked.

"I don't know, but when he comes to we are going to have a talk."

"A talk about what? You need to move back and that's that."

"Sis, I know. I just don't think you understand how I feel about him." Heather spoke out before realizing what she'd said.

"What is that supposed to mean?"

"I'm sorry. I didn't mean to say that."

Heather felt like she put her foot in her mouth by dismissing Justice's feelings about her dead fiancé. The conversation was starting to go south.

"I know you didn't mean it, but I am only trying to protect you. The next time something happens, it could be you."

"You don't have to remind me."

"Then I won't. Get your butt back here or I'll be out there to get you."

Heather heard someone come inside the bathroom. She sat still and didn't say anything in response to Justice's demand.

"Do you hear me?" Justice asked.

Heather didn't respond. The person who came into the bathroom wasn't moving into a stall. They seemed to have stayed at the door.

"Heather?" Justice called out.

Heather was still silent.

"What is going on? Do you hear me?"

The person started to walk toward Heather's stall. She was very still and didn't move. She looked at the lock to make sure it was latched on the stall. Justice was still trying to get Heather to respond to her. Heather disconnected the call. The footsteps became closer. The stall next to Heather opened and closed. Then at her stall the person grabbed the handled and pulled the locked door. It startled her.

"Heather." A man's voice said.

"Who's there?" Heather said.

"It's Milestone. Are you okay?"

"My goodness, you scared the shit out of me."

"Come out. Let's go." Milestone staid.

Within seconds of Heather coming out, Milestone's phone rang.

"Hello?" He said on speakerphone.

"Where the hell are you? I think Heather is in trouble? I was just talking to her…" Justice rambled.

"Calm down, sis. I have her."

"You do? Let me speak to her." Justice demanded.

"Go ahead, you're on speaker." Milestone said.

"Hello." Heather said.

"Don't ever scare me like that again!" Justice yelled.

"Don't you yell at me! I was scared myself. I didn't know who came in the bathroom."

"I am glad that you are with Milestone. He's good people and will make sure that you straight."

"We're leaving now. I'll keep you posted." Heather said.

"I am going to make sure you get a flight out of LA by tomorrow. I am not taking no for an answer."

"I will leave after Mark is out of the woods.

Besides, I still have work out here."

"I am not hearing of you staying pass tomorrow."

Heather knew there was no arguing with her best friend. She had to agree to even get her off the phone.

Milestone pulled up at The Ritz in Downtown LA. Since she did not get a chance to make other arrangements, she had to trust his choice.

"I would normally not stay in such a crowded hotel." Heather finally said.

"I have my reason. If I didn't think it was safe, then I wouldn't have brought you here." Milestone said.

"OK."

Heather opened the door to the 2-bedroom suite and found her way to the master bathroom. She closed the door behind her. She seemed to stay in there quite a long time.

"Are you alright in there?" Milestone asked

through the crease of the door.

"I am. I needed to decompress for a minute."

"Okay. Take your time. I am headed to my room, Let me know if you need anything." He said.

After her shower, Heather thought about booking her flight, but she couldn't bring herself to do it. There was so much unfinished business. It was not like her to leave a situation unsettled, but the lifestyle that Mark lived was not the life she wanted. Heather couldn't ask him to choose. That wouldn't be fair.

CHAPTER ELEVEN

It took another few weeks before Mark was released from the hospital. The poisonous substance had caused damage to his lungs which caused pneumonia. Heather kept the B-Side schedule going and had started to feel like danger was no longer around her because Mark no longer around her. That was bad to think, but it was true. Milestone was still keeping tabs on her, but they were not staying together at the same hotel suite. He went back to his place, but stopped by at least twice a week to check on her. Justice accepted that

Heather was going to do whatever she wanted to do, so she stopped badgering her to move back to the east coast.

Heather's visits to see Mark were less and less the closer it got to him being released. On the day he would check out, it had been a couple of days since she went to visit him. The hospital had to move him several time because of the fans who managed to find him.

"All ready to go?" Heather said with her purse still on her arm.

"You have no idea. I want to get the hell out of here." Mark said.

"Then let's go." Heather said.

Mark was already dressed and ready. The paperwork was complete and he was as free as a bird.

"Are we going back to your place?" Mark asked.

"Actually, I am going to drop you off at a

studio condo that I rented for you. It's in the same community as mine."

"What? Why? I don't want to live in a studio?"

"You don't have a choice. All of your so called people have stopped working for you because they thought that you were basically going to die. So, I have managed your affairs as best I can. It's not like I had access to your accounts to find you something better."

"What about the beach house?" He suggested.

"The lease was up and besides; I haven't stayed there since the incident."

"But we are engaged."

"We were engaged."

"I thought we squashed that when you squirted all over the kitchen floor."

"Nice try! But this last incident is just the reason why I can't go through with this wedding. Someone is still trying to hurt you and the people around you. If you don't care about my safety and keeping me out of this, then I don't know what else to say."

"Are you questioning my intentions? I would never do anything that would jeopardize your safety."

"I have already decided. I am moving back to New York as soon as we close out post production."

"You don't have to wait until the film is over. I will handle the rest of it. Besides, it's my money."

"Oh, it's your money! Really?! That's how you're going to end this? You're going to remind me that you have all the money invested in this project."

"I didn't mean it like that."

"It's too late. I took it that way. I am going to drop you off and I'll be on my way."

Heather and Mark rode to the condo in silence. She was pissed that he would actually throw his money into the conversation as if that ever mattered to her. Even though she knew it was his emotions talking, she did not cut him any slack. That was a low blow and she didn't deserve that.

♠♠♠

Mark and Heather worked closely together on post production and packaging. Building the soundtrack was yet more proof that they were a one-of-a-kind team. They spent many late nights debating and blending their genius to make this movie a success.

There was no way Heather would have left prior because she had invested just as much as Mark did. He may have paid for it, but it was her writing that made the story come alive.

The day they sealed their distribution and film release deal, Mark invited the cast to his studio for a little celebration. Heather tried to skip the festivities, but she had grown attached to the crew and did not want to spoil the fun. As the evening progressed, music blared in the background, everyone seemed to be having a good time, including Heather.

"Shots!" Mark yelled.

The crew cheered and everyone took their glass and chugged their shot. After a few of those the crew was in full party mode. They danced, played card games, and even did a little karaoke. It was a really good time. It was well after 2 am before the last guest left. Heather had made herself comfortable on the sofa.

"I'll help you clean up." Heather offered trying to get up from the sofa.

"Clean up? Heather, you know I have a housekeeper. She will clean up the place in the morning." Mark said.

"I should get going. I have a flight to catch tomorrow." Heather mumbled.

"I don't think so. You're not going anywhere.

You can sleep in my bed and I'll crash here on the sofa." Mark insisted.

Heather didn't move from the sofa. Mark was glad she did not have any energy to argue. He lifted her from the sofa and took her into the bedroom area.

When he laid her on the bed, he started to undress her and her eyes opened to meet his.

"What's wrong, Heather?" Marked asked.

"I'm sorry." Heather confessed.

"What are you sorry about? You haven't done anything wrong. I am the one who should be sorry."

"I feel like I have given up on you." Heather said.

"Let's get you out of these clothes." Mark said not wanting to respond to Heather's comment.

When Mark helped Heather into one of his t-shirts, she grabbed his arm before he could walk away. "Don't go."

Mark all too quickly obliged and took off his clothes and slid under the sheets with Heather. He spooned her into his embrace like he used to. His erection was inevitable. He wanted her. No matter what they were going through emotionally, she was still his. Heather did not reject him. She welcomed him inside her. Laying on their side and from the back he slid his hard shaft inside her. The position was different, but she liked it. He did all of the work. Slow, long strokes allowed his girth to reach a spot he had not touched in a while. The spot tingled from his playful taps. When she felt herself filling up with energy, he tapped her spot a few more times and she experienced a euphoric orgasm like she had never before. Mark then turned her on her back and raised her legs for more.

"I want to see your face. Open your eyes, baby."

Mark always kept his composure. He took pride in making love to Heather. Every moment mattered to him. He took his time. This time was no exception. His strokes were long and slow. He wanted to savior the feeling. When his orgasm was upon him, he leaned in close to Heather to kiss her lips. Her legs fell to his side and he pushed farther into her. She received all of him as he burst into her. He laid on her chest and then slowly fell to her side. Heather rolled into his embrace and was swiftly off to sleep.

On the flight back to New York, Heather thought about her last night with Mark. As guilty as she felt for slipping out in the morning, she felt equally as bad for having sex knowing they were not going to be together. All Heather could do was try to focus on this new phase of her life and that did not include Mark B.

Justice had rented a loft in Manhattan and told

Heather that she would not hear of her paying any rent until she found a job.

When Heather walked into the loft it was already furnished and well kept. Heather turned to Justice with curious eyes.

"How are you paying for this place?"

"I've been doing quite well so don't you worry about all that. Get back on your feet and we'll talk about you taking over the payments."

"I don't think I'll be looking for a job right away. I don't think anyone will hire me after this Mark fiasco."

"You'll get something. I will make some calls."

"You don't have to do that."

"I insist." Justice said.

"Of course." Heather conceded.

Heather knew that it was pointless to argue. Left up to Justice, Heather would be working tomorrow, but she needed some time to adjust. The life Heather knew was all jumbled up with emotions. She didn't even know if she wanted to be a writer anymore, at least not for a major publication.

Justice did not stay long after she got Heather settled in. With a view to die for, Heather went out on the terrace with her laptop and began to write.

Hours later Heather realized that she had been writing into the night. The dim light on her laptop kept her going. Her cellphone was out of reach and the busy life of New Yorkers became her background music. By the time she finished, she sat back and looked at how much she had completed. It was her first time writing freely since before she started working on Mark's tour. At that moment Heather realized that she loved writing, but not under pressure or obligation to sell or make numbers. Writing was her thing and it mattered to her that she could do it at peace.

In the following weeks, Heather had completed her first manuscript for a novel. After it was finished she realized it was a mystery drama.

When she finished writing the book, she made a few calls about getting an agent. She did not want to get any help from Justice or anyone for that matter. She wanted to get her first novel published on her own. She'd got a hit.

"Heather Grand, please." A man spoke.

"This is Heather."

"Yes, this is Franco Castillo from Beefeater Publishing."

"Hi, Francis. How can I help you?"

Heather knew that she put out a few feelers for some agents, but Franco Castillo was not one of them. She knew he was phishing, but she'd hear him out.

"I came across your novel and want to represent you."

"Is that so? How did you get my information? I don't recall giving you any copies of my manuscript." Heather was matter of fact.

"I obviously have associates in the business and some of them have totally tossed your story aside, but they don't know you or your history with Mark B. James. I know you tried to cover up the story with a lot of fiction, but I was able to read right through those lines."

"And what is it that you can guarantee?" Heather inquired.

"Whooo, wait a minute. I am not making you any guarantees. I am just open to represent you and submit your manuscript to my publishing company. I am one of their top agents and I know they'll buy into the story if you let me sell it."

"Beefeater Publishing is not quite the agency that I was hoping to work with."

"Look, as I said. Those agents that you have reached out to have already laughed and tossed your book to the side. If you want to wait around for one of their calls, then be my guest."

"I'll think about it."

"If you think long, you'll think wrong. Time is money." Franco Castillo said and disconnected the line.

Heather realized that after the phone disconnected that he did not even leave his contact information. "Asshole." She said as she looked at the phone history, that said, "Unknown Caller."

For the next month, Heather wrote two other mystery novels while she waited by the phone. She was not getting any hits on her novels. She started to get discouraged and was second guessing her skills as a writer. A few rejection letters came in the mail from agents, and others never replied at all.

Eventually, she searched for the Beefeater contact as a last hope. After some research, she found out that Franco was a top agent and his specialty was mystery. She decided to give him a chance. And as he promised, he was able to sell her novels to the publisher. She got a book deal! In a quick tailspin she was back in the game. Franco became her agent and just like that she was starting a book tour.

"Our first stop is the famous New York store Books & More in two weeks." He told her.

"Sounds good."

"Are you ready to be the face of your own brand?" Franco said.

"Ready as I'll ever be."

"Alight then. Go cash that check! You're headed to the best-sellers list, my friend—I can feel it!" Franco beamed!

Heather appreciated her agent's enthusiasm. She learned to work with his all business no nonsense personality, because that's just how she liked it. But she loved when he'd get hyped up. It helped Heather believe in this new journey. So, if he said it could be done, then it could be done. So, if he felt like she had a best seller, then she believed him.

Heather was in a such different place. She and Justice were still friends, but not as close as they were before the whole Mark thing. Things were just different.

After her conference call with Franco, Heather turned on the television to watch the morning show and saw Mark on the screen promoting the film. Heather told Mark that she did not want to be involved with the promotion of the film, especially on television. She left all of that up to him. Watching Mark on television brought back feelings about him that Heather thought were long gone. It was going to be hard seeing him at the premiere that night. Heather sat with her cup of tea and watched the tail end of the interview.

"So, Mark, I understand that you're officially single these days." the show host said.

"Uh, I knew that question was coming. Well, I

really haven't put it out there that I'm single."

"The rumor is your engagement is off." She persisted.

Heather was listening intently to his response. To her, it just mattered that he still cared. She did not have to have his devotion at this point because she did not know if going back into his world was something she ever wanted to do again. She was officially old news and people had stopped asking her about Mark.

"That's the problem with the rumor mill. It is full of gossip. Heather and I are dealing with our relationship in private."

"Relationship." Both Heather and the host said at the same time.

"Well ladies, it doesn't sound like he's available." The host pouted.

The audience let out a sound of disappointment while the crease of Heather's mouth cracked into a smile.

"Mark B, we look forward to the premiere of your new film tonight, "Love Don't Make Cents", featuring Melvin Briggs and Giselle Millieon, two new heart throbs joining the scene. Thank you for coming by the Morning Show to talk with us."

"It's always a pleasure coming to the Morning Show. Thank you for having me. We'll see you tonight at the Red Carpet."

"The "Love Don't Make Cents" Red Carpet Premiere is tonight at Lincoln Theatre and will be in theatres on June 5th." The host announced.

The show cut to commercial and Heather turned off the television. Her thoughts replayed Mark's comment about how they were handling their relationship. Since he left LA, they'd only seen each other a few times. She just thought he was also ready to move on. He wasn't as persistent as he had been and Heather felt like she had to accept that.

Hours later, Heather fumbled around the apartment trying to get into the mood, but she could not. In the middle of her thoughts, there was a knock at the door. When she peeked out the hole, it was Mark. Heather unhooked the chain and opened the door.

"Hello."

"Hi, Heather. I couldn't wait until tonight to see you. Can we talk?" Marked walked in uninvited with a garment bag on his shoulder.

"Well, I was just about to start getting ready. I haven't decided what to wear yet."

"Perfect timing. I brought you something." Mark swung the garment back from his shoulder onto the tip of his finger.

"What's this?" Heather was inquisitive.

"I want us to look good on the red carpet tonight. I thought I'd pick out an outfit for you…well, my assistant did."

"Assistant? You hired someone?"

"Yes. When you left I had to get someone to help manage all of the things you were helping me with."

"What's her name?"

"His name is Arturo."

"A man?"

"Yes, a man. I didn't think I could stomach trusting another woman to handle things right now." Mark said.

"Open it up. Let's see what Arturo picked out for me." Heather insisted.

"I hope you like it."

Mark opened the garment bag and revealed the most beautiful sequin dress. It was a floor length off the shoulder dress with blue and black sequin with specks of silver.

"It's beautiful."

"I'm glad you like it. So what time should I pick you up tonight?"

"Pick me up?" Heather was confused.

"We are stepping out on that carpet together." Mark insisted.

"Oh, we are?"

"Damn, right. We deserve this moment."

"Alrighty then, I should be ready by 6."

"Okay, I'll be here."

"Thanks, Mark." Heather said and stepped up on her tip toes and planted a kiss on his cheek.

"The cheek? It's like that?"

"Don't start." Heather threw a love tap on his chest.

"Okay, okay. I'll be nice."

"You better be! Now get out so I can start getting ready."

"One more thing. Hair and make-up are on their way up to add the finishing touches."

"You're too much!"

"Anything for you." Mark said and this time he placed a soft kiss on Heather's lips before he turned and left her apartment.

A couple hours later, both hair and make-up artists were finalizing their touches. By the time 6 o'clock rolled around, Heather was transformed into a beautiful queen.

The door bell rang at 6 pm sharp. The hair and make up artists were packing up and ready to depart. When Heather opened the door it was Mark.

"Damn." He said looking at Heather.

"Hi, Mark."

"You are so beautiful."

"Thank you."

"It will be an honor to escort you to our premiere tonight."

Mark grabbed Heather by the hand and escorted her out of the apartment.

"Lock up the place and I'll see you ladies at the event." Mark said to the artists who were still cleaning up.

"Here is the key and thanks so much." Heather said as she let the door close behind her.

When the limo pulled up to the event it was swarming with fans and movie goers. The marque was plastered with the film title, "Love Don't Makes Cents" and the presenters' names Mark B. James and Heather Grand.

"Wow. You put my name on the marque."

"Of course, baby. I couldn't have done this without you."

"Awww, this is such a surprise."

Before opening the door, Mark grabbed Heather's hand, "I know this isn't the best time to tell you this, but the reason I know I love you is because you made me realize that I don't want anything else in this world if I can't have you to share it with."

"What are you saying?" Heather said with a tear forming in her eye.

"I'm saying that I got some changes to make."

"What kind of changes, Mark? I don't want you to give up music if that is what you love to do."

"It's not that simple, Heather. I never realized how much I loved you until you were gone. Like you were gone...gone. Three thousand miles away, gone. I've dreaded every day without you by my side. I can still do what I love. I have no limits, you know this. I have many ideas and when I was with you those ideas were coming to life."

"Mark, I don't want you to give up your music career to be with me. What would that look like?" Heather chuckled at his ridiculous statements and wiped the tear before it ruined her make up.

"I haven't given up on us. You may have thought I did, but I will show you that all of this has been an eye opening experience. I laid in the hospital twice and almost dead both times and you were there for me. No entourage, no executives, and even the fans faded. I had no one, only you. My contract ended with Retrospect Records last month and I have already started making the changes I need to—for myself."

Heather looked out the limo window at the screaming fans who could not wait to lay their eyes on Mark. She looked at him and then at the fans and smiled, "All of those screaming fans are for you."

"We can pull off right now and go in the back door for all I care. I don't need those fans, I need you."

Heather's heart melted. She couldn't help it. It was her love for him that wouldn't let go no matter how much time had spanned between them. She loved him from day one and there was no changing that.

"Let's go." Heather said and took in a deep breath and tapped on the window for the driver to open the door.

All of the fans went crazy when they saw Mark walk on the red carpet. The were groping trying to touch him and take pictures, but he just kept walking with Heather right by his side.

Inside the theatre Heather saw her family sitting in the front row. It was the most beautiful sight to see all of the people who loved her all in one room. They both greeted Aunt Mae, Heather's family, and Justice.

Before the premiere started, Mark took the mic and introduced the film, "Ladies and Gentlemen, thank you for joining us tonight. I see so many familiar faces in the room and some new supporters. This is my first film and I couldn't have done it without the help of my best friend, Heather Grand," the crowd erupted in cheer, "This movie is a testament of how two people can come from two different worlds and be made perfect for each other. So without further or due, I present to you, "Love Don't Make Cents.""

Mark joined Heather in the audience to watch the movie. He held her hand throughout and once even leaned over and kissed her on the ear. Heather tingled inside and smiled trying to watch the movie.

Before the credits rolled, someone came to get Mark from the audience, "I'll be right back."

"Okay." Heather nodded and kept her eyes on the screen.

Moments later the credits were ready to roll and the crowd erupted in cheer. Mark made his way back up to the stage and waved for the cast to join him. "Come up, everyone and take your bow."

The cast joined Mark and Heather on the stage to receive the applause from the audience. After the audience calmed down Mark made another announcement.

"To all of my fans and supporters, it has been an interesting ride as a hip hop artist in this industry. I've become my own man because of your support, but I have to say that this last year with two near death experiences have opened up my eyes. I love music, but it's time for me to focus on a few other things that are more important."

Mark looked down the line of actors and actresses and found Heather. He went to her in front of everyone and got down on one knee. The audience gasped in awe at what they knew was about to happen. One of the actors held the mic for Mark to speak into so the audience could hear his every word.

"Heather, I haven't been able to give you all that you deserve and I want to make it right. I miss you and I will not leave this theatre without you. I want you be my wife. Will you marry me?"

Heather's seemingly new fan base screamed in excitement at the proposal. The entire place seemed to be drowned out as they stood in ovation. Heather could only see Mark in front of her with hope and desire in his eyes. Knowing what she wanted, he was really willing to give up his crazy lifestyle to be happy with her.

"Yes, Mark. Yes, I will marry you." Heather

said.

Mark put a ring on her finger, a bigger diamond than the first time. Heather looked at it and couldn't help, but to tear up. The audience cheered even louder when Mark stood up and picked up his woman and kissed her while twirling her around. The moment was even more surreal as the first time he asked her to marry him. Heather couldn't wake up from this dream because it wasn't a dream. Mark was her man in real life and that was just the way it was going to be.

At the premiere after party everyone congratulated the couple, except Justice. She was acting weird, but Heather tried to brush it off so that it didn't ruin her moment. Heather's sister Tiffany finally got to meet Mark and she was overly excited to take pictures with him to share with her friends. Heather's parents and Aunt Mae found a quiet corner to sit down and observe the festivities.

"Mark, you never talk about your father. Where

is he?" Heather asked sipping a glass of sparkling water.

"I never met my father. He ran out on my mom when she was pregnant and she never got a chance to tell him about me before she died." Mark said unmoved.

"Oh, I'm so sorry."

"Don't be. I can't miss someone I never knew. My mom and Aunt Mae did me well." Mark was proudly.

"Indeed they did." Heather tapped her glass against his.

As the party started to wind down, Heather found herself feeling a little tired.

"It's time to go babe. You look exhausted."

"I know, but not until I talk to Justice." Heather said, "Where is she?"

Heather looked around the room until she saw Justice talking to some guy. She stormed over to her best friend to let her have it.

"Justice, I need to talk to you." Heather said firmly standing up to her friend.

"Not now. I'm busy." Justice ignored Heather and focused on the guy.

"Yes, now. Beat it!" Heather said to the guy who looked like a groupie.

"What the hell are you doing? What do you want?" Justice was annoyed.

"I noticed that you've been a little stand offish lately. What's wrong with you?"

"Look, do what you want. You were safely out of his web, but somehow you find a way to get back in it. If you want to be killed in the crossfire, then that's your problem, not mine."

"What are you talking about?"

"You're so naïve Heather. Go and be with your man. I'm happy for you, really...I am."

"Why are you acting so upset? I don't understand why you're doing this." Heather said.

"Just watch your own back from now on. I am

done babysitting you." Justice said and put her glass on the bar and walked out.

Mark saw the end of the exchange and came over, "What was that all about?"

"I don't know. She seems to think that I am still in danger being with you."

"What is she talking about?" Mark asked looking in Justice's direction.

"She thinks it's not over."

"Heather, we have a flight to catch as soon as we leave this premiere. I am not wasting another minute talking about Justice and her crazy theories." Mark tried to brush off Heather's statement.

"What flight? What are you talking about?"

"It was supposed to be a surprise, but I feel like I need to ease your anxiety that we're going to be okay."

"We're leaving to get married? But what about my family?"

"Don't worry, sweetie. Don't worry. As a matter of fact, let's slip out the back. Our folks have already left."

"Look at you." Heather cracked a smile.

"I told you, I've got this. Now, let's go."

Heather followed Mark's lead out the back of the theatre. His new security team, that came highly recommended, was already standing at the door waiting for the couple to approach.

"Boss, are we set?" The body guard said.

"Yes, Chase, let's get the hell out of here."

Chase opened the door of the theatre and made sure the car was ready to take off. He escorted the couple to the back of the SUV and once inside they took off.

It felt like they were driving off into the sunset. The lit skyline of New York City was fading into the background as they drove to LaGuardia to catch their flight.

"Where are we going?" Heather asked.

"It's a secret. No one knows except those who will be there."

"Why is it a secret from me?" Heather pouted.

"Okay, it's a surprise for you. There's a difference." Mark teased.

Heather tussled and played with Mark in the backseat on the way to the airport. She tickled him trying to get him to crack. He laughed harder than she ever heard him before. It was kind of sexy, she thought. It made her unbuckle her seatbelt and straddled him.

"What are you doing?" Mark asked as he received Heather's seductive advancements.

Heather did not reply. She continued to slow grind on his lap and Mark hit the partition button. It closed slowly. When it was closed Heather unbuckled Mark's pants and lifted her dress and finagled out of her thong panties. Mark was still silent as he made his way under he long dress. He held on tightly to Heather while sliding his hand down her waist to get to her ass. Mark's shaft was firm and at attention when Heather mounted it. She let out a soft moan and rode his manhood in long deep strokes. Her hand gripped the seat back and the lights from the streets caught the sparkle in her exquisite diamond ring. He missed her. She could feel it in his energy. Mark held Heather close and smothered his face into her breast. With each slow grind, Heather's clit rubbed against Marks stubble happy trail. He grabbed her face and kissed her deeply. They didn't speak any words to each other. They didn't make a sound. The intensity in their movements spoke for them. Heather didn't want to climax, but she felt it coming. Mark pulled Heather closer as his grinds became slower and harder. He knew his woman. He knew her climax was near. He could feel her electrifying muscles squeezing the life right out of him. Mark was ready to join her. He waited…she grinded…then they came. Heather gushed creamy juices that competed with Mark's thick and milky cum. The two had their first silent orgasm. Mark kissed Heather intensely, "I am so in love with you." He said.

"Hmmmm." Heather moaned while holding Mark's head against her fast beating heart.

"And I'm still not going to tell you where we're going." Mark whispered.

"It's okay, my love. I don't care where we go, as long as I am with you."

♠ ♠ ♠

When they reached the tarmac for take off, Heather asked Mark about her family, "Will they meet us there?"

"Yes. I've confirmed they're already in the air. I didn't book the family and our luggage on the jet. Everyone will meet us there. So, go ahead back and get you some rest. We have a busy day tomorrow."

"And what are you going to do?" Heather

asked.

"I have some emails to send out and then I'll be in there to join you." Mark said.

Heather didn't ask anymore questions. She knew Mark had it under control. He always did.

♠♠♠

The next morning Heather woke up to the sound of the pilot announcement. Mark was still curled up in a ball, she nudged him.

"Yeah!" Mark shot up from the bed as if he heard the word, "Fire!"

"It's okay, baby. We're about to land." Heather assured him.

"Oh, shit. You scared the shit out of me." Mark said.

When the pilot made his final announcement, Mark sat up on the bed and put on a jogging suit he laid out the night before.

"I put this out for you to put on until we get into the hotel." Mark pointed to the outfit next to his.

Heather slowly got out of bed and made her way to the bathroom to freshen up. Mark was already dressed when she came out to put on her clothes.

"So where are we?" Heather asked.

"It's still a surprise until we get off the plane and no peeking." Mark said closing the shade.

The two of them took their seats for landing. Heather had butterflies while maintaining her composure. Mark was smiling watching Heather squirm in her seat.

"Soon, sweetheart. Soon you'll be Mrs. James." Mark teased.

"Is that so?" Heather tossed a first class pillow in his direction. Mark caught it and smiled. He was enjoying the idea of surprising Heather with their wedding day. It was the best day he could dream up.

The view was amazing. A private ceremony at the top of the Eifel Tower at sunset was nothing Heather could have imagined. Heather's immediate family and Aunt Mae were in attendance. Everyone she loved was there except her best friend, Justice. It saddened her to think that on such a special day she wasn't there. It was what they talked about as kids. Having a dream wedding with their dream guy. This was surely a dream come true.

"Oh, Heather it was such a beautiful ceremony."

"Thanks mother." Heather said kissing her mother on the cheek.

Mark joined his new wife and mother-in-law before they could break up their little chat.

"You'd better take care of our baby." Heather's mom said just as her father walked up.

"It is my sole mission." Mark affirmed and shook Mr. Grand's hand.

The reception was moved to the private restaurant inside the Eifel Tower. When the couple and the family arrived, they were greeted with some of the industries most elite celebrities.

"Introducing Mr. and Mrs. Mark B. James!" announced DJ Kadee.

"Congratulations!" The guests yelled when the couple came in preceded by the family.

The reception was as special as it could be. Heather saw Mandy with her man and Mr. Fleuron from Musiq Magazine sitting at a table. She saw the CEO of Retrospect Records at another table, her film cast and crew were seated together, and to her surprise, Justice sat at a table with a guy that Heather didn't recognize.

The newlyweds sat at the head table surrounded by the family. The new security detail stood around the edges of the table and the exits.

They blended in well with their tuxedos. As the festivities started, Mark took a moment to thank everyone for coming. He tapped on his champagne glass to get the room silent.

"Can I have your attention, please." Mark cleared his throat, "I want to say, this has been one of the most amazing rollercoaster rides of my life. I have been through a lot in the past year with this woman." Mark looked down at Heather and continued, "It was never the fame or even my little fortune that made her stay, it was just me. I have inherited a family marrying this woman and I look forward to a future with her. Cheers." The room erupted in applause.

Heather took the spoon and tapped on her own glass. Mark was surprised as she kept a hold of his hand so that he could stand with her.

"I am not much of a public speaker, so I'll keep this short. Mark is right, I do love him for much more than his fame, I love him for the man he has always been to me from day one." She looked in his eyes, "It will be my honor to grow old and raise a family with you by my side." Heather mouthed, "I'm pregnant."

Mark couldn't contain himself. He picked Heather up in her gown and kissed her with so much passion. She couldn't hold back any tears. He put her down and Heather said to him, "Surprise."

"Oooh, you got me! Can I tell them, babe?" Mark whispered as the crowd was still applauding their speeches. Heather nodded.

"Hey everyone, we're gonna have a baby!" Mark yelled.

It was a standing ovation. The family stood and Heather's mother came over and gave Heather the biggest hug.

"It's time to celebrate! DJ Kadee, let's get this party started." Mark yelled.

Family and friends joined in the celebration.

"Congratulations are in order times two."

Justice said as she approached Heather on the dance floor.

"I wanted to tell you when I found out, but things just haven't been the same between us, you know..." Heather said.

"I know. I was a little jealous of you and I didn't want to admit it." Justice said.

"Well, the last thing I wanted to do was flaunt Mark in your face. Both of our men were shot that night. I felt so bad that Darrin was killed."

"I've come to grips with what happened to Darrin. You know I only wanted you to be safe no matter what." Justice said.

"Thank you." Heather said.

"I am just happy that you're in another chapter in your lives. Congratulations on your book deal. You thought I didn't know." Justice said finally.

"Again, since we haven't been talking, I didn't bring it up, but thank you. The last 24 hours was not planned, but we'll catch up back in New York."

"Mark told me about the plans last minutes, so for you, I couldn't miss it. Besides, it's a great story!" Justice teased rubbing her BFFs belly.

Mark walked up, "Have we kissed and made up, yet?" Mark stood between the girls.

Heather looked over at Justice, "Yes, we've ironed things out."

"Good, cause we're going to need a babysitter, soon!" Mark pulled Justice in a little closer and hugged her tightly around her neck.

"Babysitter my ass! I don't do babies and Heather knows it." Justice jabbed Mark in the ribs to let go of her neck.

Mark felt the tinge in his rib from her more than friendly tap. Mark knew about Justice, but he knew she wouldn't hurt him or Heather, especially now. Heather was just enjoying the moment she thought was genuine and he wanted to keep it that way. As they say, 'keep your friends close, but your enemies closer'. Mark had his eye on Justice and she knew it.

EPILOGUE

"Breaking News! Police have made another arrest in the nearly two-year old murder case of Attorney Darrin Fischer and attempted murder of rapper Mark B. James." Justice said.

"Babe! Come quick." Heather yelled.

"What is it?" Mark came quickly with his infant son in his arms.

They watched the news and saw the police escorting Manny, Brandon, and Gabriella into the courthouse.

"I still can't believe Manny would sell you out

for money." Heather was disappointed.

"Money changes people and so does a little power." Mark said rocking his son to sleep.

"I guess it's hard to trust anyone."

"It is. But since I've left the limelight, I haven't felt like I needed to worry about all that."

"You're still Mark B. James to the world, honey."

"True, but I am more like a husband and father to you and MJ now...that's boring news. The rest of the world don't have nothing on you two." Mark sat on the sofa next to his wife with his son sound asleep on his chest.

The house that Mark built for his new family was just off the coast of Key West, FL. He wanted a new start in a secluded tropical city. What better place to go than South Florida? They were far enough from all of the people and elements, but close enough to still make things happen.

Heather was a stay at home mom and spent a

lot of time working on writing film projects and her next best selling novel. Mark B. was in and out of Miami working with new artists and when he craved the stage, he would do concerts other special events. The glue they started over two years ago was still intact, B-Side Productions. Their film was such a success that they landed their first network deal for a drama series of which they were co-show runners.

Heather never saw that strange man since that day in L.A. The dark cloud that was hovering over her and Mark had dissipated. Heather felt positive energy around her little family. The Universe had answered and love was starting to make sense now.

"We did all of this for nothing, you idiots!" Justice scolded her enterprise.

The group of thugs sat around a makeshift executive table in a dingy, dimly lit room. Justice wore a face that she had never shown on television. She was a mean bitch.

"But boss...he..." A heavy set thug spoke up.

"Don't—but boss me! That motha fucka was supposed to be dead twice and look at him now. That was a two for one deal. Now his ass ain't worth the contract we had on him."

"We still got our eye on him." Another thug spoke.

"For what? We can't do shit now with my godson in the house. He needs his father, asshole! We have to move on. I have a new target and this time you better not fuck up or all of your asses are dead."

"Who is the target?" The slimmer thug asked.

"Henry St. Germaine with his snitch ass. He

knows too much." Justice said.

###

ABOUT THE AUTHOR

V. Marie was born and raised in Columbus, Ohio. V. Marie remembers writing her first book in grade school, titled, "All About Me". The book made with colored paper, affixed by Elmer's® glue, tape, staples and written in pencil, is in a box, still intact as a reminder of how early talents are born. Poems and love letters from high school fill other boxes to support her belief in love and the never-ending possibility of happiness. Who would have ever thought that 35+ years later, she would be sharing that talent with the world.

V. Marie hopes that you have become a fan of life *for life*. That is the ultimate message – fear nothing. She believes that life is meant to be lived and you will either live it vivaciously – or not and happiness; which is a state of mind, you will either BE – or not. You get to choose.

V. Marie resides in South Florida where she enjoys the natural elements provided by the Atlantic Ocean, her sanctuary. A student of life, V. Marie enjoys writing about love, relationships, and life in general.

If you have enjoyed "Love Don't Make Cents", then check out her senior novel, "Love, Fire & Ice" and sequel "Love on Fire". V. Marie would love to hear your review on the website at AuthorVMarie.com or by email at: AuthorVMarie@gmail.com.

47160CB00002B/421